PETER LAMBERT

INVOLVED BY ACCIDENT III
INTO THE SUNSET

Printed in the United States of America
Library of Congress Control Number: 2025919468
ISBN: Softcover   978-1-969213-06-9
     e-Book   978-1-969213-07-6
Republished by: TwinVerse Prime
Publication Date: 09/08/2025

To order copies of this book, contact:
TwinVerse Prime
Phone: (725) 257-6538
clients@twinverseprime.com
www.twinverseprime.com/

Table of Contents

Foreword

Some seven years have passed since Stephen Leigh-Grace became involved by accident in rescuing Shamir and David from being attacked by the river side as he was moving his boat *Finbar ll* down the river ready to begin another years cruising with his family and then suffering an attack himself. While he was in hospital he met and ultimately fell in love with one of the detectives investigating that case, Nita Patel. The following year more drama, when he became involved again in exposing an international gang, trafficking young girls, alcohol and drugs across Europe and the UK eventually assisting UK and European immigration and custom authorities in detaining the gang both here in the UK and through the Low countries. Finally, while returning across the channel from the family's summer vacation cruising around Northern France, more drama again when they went to the aid a family whose yacht had been disabled in a sudden storm.

 Since then life has been relatively simple and quiet for him, Nita and the family. His daughter Emma went through university gaining her degree in engineering. During her time at Manchester she met Angus and they married quite soon after leaving Uni and they now have twins. This is the last book of the trilogy, read on and see how it all turns out for them.

Chapter One

Sunday morning, late September, outside there's still evidence from autumns first frost lingering on the car roofs and on the dark sides of the house roofs across the street yet to be kissed by the sun's rays. The small lounge of Stephens's house is brightly lit by the glare of the autumn sun streaming through the window; the radio plays quietly in the background tuned into the local FM station. They sit, Stephen in his favourite chair holding the weekend paper he's just lowered to look at Nita, she's sitting on the little settee across the room her feet drawn up reading the supplement from the paper. He sighs, that attracts her attention.

'What?'

'Mmm nothing I was just thinking its seven years since we met you know.'

'So, it's not been a jail sentence has it?' she answers looking at him quizzically, 'why mention it now particularly?'

He chuckles, 'No, but I was just thinking I'm not feeling itchy!'

Looking really confused now she says.

'Stephen… I haven't a clue what you are babbling about!'

Chuckling again he replies, '

'There's a saying about relationships when they reach seven years, it's called the seven-year itch.'

She rotates a wrist to hurry up his explanation, 'And?'

'Well here we are seven years into this relationship and I can't think of being with or spending time with anyone else but you. When I think back to where I was, where my life was, then you walked into my hospital room and… well here I am, so much in love with you I cannot imagine a day not spending time with you or talking to you, particularly when I'm away through the week.'

She settles back into the cushions of the settee watching him steadily, thinking, he returns to reading the paper. She stands suddenly moving to the kitchen, 'Tea, Coffee?'

Glancing over the top of the paper smiling.

'Please sugar, can I have a cafetiere please'

She stops at the door looking back at him, tuts saying.

'You're going to want hot milk with that I suppose… hmm?'

Nodding, 'Please.'

'You take me for granted sometimes you know I obviously spoiled you at the beginning!'

She leaves the lounge shaking her head. Fifteen minutes later she places a tray with two mugs and a small jug of warm milk on it plus a plate of biscuits. Passing a mug to Stephen she turns picks up hers and sits on the settee again.

'This run you're doing next week, how long will you be away?'

Putting the paper to one side he takes a drink from his mug.

'Ohh that's good, thank you.' then reply's, 'I should be back in ten days, I'm only doing Holland then into Germany ending up with a home run from somewhere near Strasbourg to a place in Sheffield, then home.'

'Tell me again why you? You've not done Europe for nearly two years or more?'

With a hint of a smile he says.

'The lad that usually does that Euro run is on maternity leave.'

Nita squeals with laughter, 'He's on what…!'

'Well paternity leave then… you know what I meant!'

She continues chuckling as he continues.

'The other driver who's done that run is on holiday so because I've done continental in the past and since I've spent some time in the office this last year doing some of the planning I know where these drops are so the boss asked if I'd do it. The other drivers out in Europe now are way up north and not due back for another two weeks or more.'

'This isn't the thin edge of the wedge to get you back on those Scan-Euro runs you were doing when we met is it?'

'Oh no definitely not! If the boss hadn't made this worth my while, I'd not be doing it. Nita, I'm getting a month's money for ten days work then a week's paid leave on top… It's a no brainer, honestly.'

'Okay, it's just that it's been so long since you've been away for so long, I'm going to find it hard to do the home alone thing again; you know what I mean, the Skype calls at night? The other thing is since you've been on home runs there's been no getting involved in other people's problems! God forbid, I'm getting too old to deal with you being a superhero again do you understand?'

Nodding, 'Totally sugar, you and me both, I'm not sure my old ribs would stand another kicking!'

Gently massaging his side. Getting up from his chair he disappears into the kitchen.

'Do you want more tea sugar?'

'No I'm good thanks.'

Returning to the lounge he sits beside her, taking her hand and looking into her eyes as he says quietly.

'This seven years has been absolutely amazing, you were so right about me and how I'd just stepped of the round-about after Suzanne's death. I know we've talked over the why's and how's again and again but that first weekend on *Finbar* was the stuff of romantic novels and we've not got to the end yet have we?'

Leaning against his shoulder she scrunches up her nose.

'I got such a buzz from that weekend, I'm sorry but I really felt so naughty. The challenge of bedding you just got to me I wanted you so so much. Remember 'The Graduate'? Well I was Mrs Robinson that weekend and oh did I love the roll! What I didn't bank on was starting to fall in love with you. Your first trip away after that weekend was hell, I'd tasted the honey and then it was away… gone.' kissing his cheek she continues, 'Do you remember what I said to you as you turned for home about not being tired?'

'Oh yes, I was…'

She interrupts him.

'I couldn't wait to get my hands on you again, how does that saying go… something about leaving them wanting more!'

They finish the sentence in unison, 'Leave them wanting more!'

Laughing together at their impromptu duet he takes her in his arms and kisses her, she responds returning the kiss. Separating, but only inches apart he says.

'We haven't sorted anything for dinner tonight; so lovely lady, option one lunch at the Duchess; option two fish and chips or option three a takeaway later?'

'Oh decisions decisions, it's Sunday I shouldn't have to make decisions at the weekend. There could be a fourth option you know,' stroking his inner thigh she raises an eyebrow. 'It's good for the diet and the waistline too. What do you want?'

Looking at her hand gently stroking his thigh, then into her brown eyes he sees the expression he knows only too well and smirks.

'Hmmm, you're just insatiable lady...'

'Look, you're going away for two weeks nearly, I'm going to have to resort to hugging my bear and talking to him at night, so I need to get as much of you as I can and store you up for the long nights alone... Oh the pain.'

She says becoming dramatic, swooning and holding the back of her hand against her forehead.

'All alone... night after night... cold and terrified at what goes bump in the night!'

She stops, sheepishly looking at him under her hand to see his reaction. Seeing she's failed to get one, she slumps back against the settee cushions pouting. Nonchalantly he stretches across to the coffee table and passes her the box of tissues; patting her leg he says.

'You know it will be hell for me too sugar, huddled up in my tiny bunk, who knows what dangers could befall me... abduction, highway robbery just for starters! Maybe you should come with me and ride shot gun!'

Suddenly enthused at the thought, she sits bolt upright.

'Oh yeah, you said I could come sometime, I'll ring the sarge and see if I can get the time off!'

'Okay but haven't you got that court appearance at the end of the week with Alan Syms.'

'Bummer! It's important too, we've taken weeks making the case for the CPS to prosecute.'

Stroking her shoulder sympathetically he says.

'I've said I will take you with me and one day and I will… promise.'

Shrugging her shoulders and smiling.

'That's the only missing bit of us, our love and the passion. I want to make love to you in your truck,' giggling a little, 'then I've got four aces, a full house.'

They laugh and kiss.

'Okay so what are we doing for food?' he asks.

'Duchess, the Sunday roast and all the bits.'

Leaving her sitting on the settee he goes into the hall to return moments later with their coats.

'Hold your horses Ferryman I need to sort my face out, I'm not going out looking like I've just crawled out of my pit. Five minutes… well there abouts.'

Kissing him quickly as she passes him in the door; he watches her run up the stairs.

Walking through the ornate entrance to the Duchess and up to the bar, they stand waiting, a young girl, a sixth former from the high school working to add to her allowance, passes them carrying a tray of food.

'Hiya, are you wanting to eat?'

Nita replies, 'Please.'

Stopping for a moment she asks. 'In the bar or restaurant?'

Nita looks at Stephen, then says. 'Not fussed, where you can fit us.'

'Okay, give me a minute, I'll get you two menus.'

Turning to the bar Stephen nods to three guys grouped at one end. One of them acknowledges the pair.

'Alright you two?' then to Stephen says, 'when you off again?'

Stephen smiles, 'Yeah we're good thanks, actually I'm out on Tuesday for about a week and a bit.'

The man nods, returning to his conversation with his friends.

'Drink?' Stephen asks.

'A glass of red please.'

Looking at her momentarily, 'Red?'

'Please.'

'Okay… reds not your usual tipple.'

'So… I'm having the beef and a nice glass of red will be just perfect.'

He shrugs, turning back to the bar as someone says 'Hello.' He sees Jean the landlady smiling at him, then looking round his bulk to see Nita she says.

'Hello duck, you both alright?'

'Fine thanks, fancied lunch out as he's off again. I need a treat to prepare myself for being deserted!'

'Quite right mi-duck, quite right.'

'Right,' Stephen says decisively, 'a large house red and a pint of lager please.'

As Jean pours their drinks she asks.

'Seen anything of Mick recently?'

Stephen shakes his head, passing Nita her drink.

'No, last I heard was he'd gone to somewhere in Lincolnshire to stay with his brother. That was maybe three or four months ago.'

Jeans nods, 'We heard that too; it's not the same without him propping up the bar in an evening.'

Smiling broadly she adds, 'My takings have taken a dive since he left…! I'll put these on your bill okay?'

Stephen nods, 'Thanks.'

Jean calls to the young waitress en-route to the kitchen with her hands full of plates and serving dishes.

'Poppy, find a table for these two please,'

The girl nods, disappears momentarily into the kitchen to return saying to them.

'Follow me.'

She leads them to a table set in the curved area of the bay window at the front of the pub.

'Will this be alright?'

'Fine thanks.'

Nita slides in one side of the table Stephen the other, the waitress hands them a menu each telling them. 'The soup is spicy vegetable.'

She turns and walks away towards another empty table and begins to clear it.

'Beef for you then and I think I'll go with the pork.'

Attracting Poppy's attention he orders their meals, taking a drink he begins to say.

'Thinking what Jean just said, I've been wondering how Mick has been. I'd like to catch up with him one evening to see how he's doing. It can't be easy facing up to the fact that the job you've had since leaving school just ends. I'd feel useless, let down wouldn't you?'

Nodding, she replies

'It must have knocked him for six, they didn't give him much notice really but he's not been moping around bless him, he could've spent all his time in here drinking himself to death or down at the Indian piling on the pounds. All credit to him he's picked himself up and gone 'walkabout', I wonder when he last saw his brother.'

Shrugging he begins to say something when Poppy comes to their table with their meals on a tray and a tureen of vegetables and a gravy boat. Placing it on an adjoining table, she takes the roast beef dinner and sets it before Nita, turns and picking up the roast pork places it in front of Stephen, finally she puts the vegetables and gravy boat in the centre of their table.

'Would you like any sauces or mustard?'

Shaking her head Nita says, 'No thanks.'

'Have you any apple sauce?' Stephen asks.

'Sure.' she replies, crossing to the large dresser at the back of the bar returning with a ramekin of sauce to the table. 'Enjoy your meals.'

They both eat without talking until Stephen picks up a piece of the pork crackling and bites into it, it shatters and he begins to crunch it. Nita looks across the table at him shaking her head slightly.

'Do you think you could crunch quietly it sounds like a cement mixer full of stones?'

Grinning broadly at her, he replies.

'Hmm, sorry sugar this is the best bit, I never seem to be able to get my crackling like this; a bit like my Yorkshires they never quite seem to rise like the restaurant ones do.'

'Well crunch quietly or I'm moving tables… okay!'

Finishing the last forkful of his food, he looks at Nita.

'Got room for a pudding?'

Shaking her head, 'You must be joking I'm stuffed, that was so lovely.'

Poppy comes across to their table.

'Everything alright, have you finished?'

'Lovely thanks Poppy, could I have a look at the sweet menu please.'

Leaving the table, her arms full of plates and the tureen she disappears through the door to the kitchen, returning moments later and handing Stephen the menu card. Studying it for a moment he nods then glancing at Nita he offers it to her to look at, shaking her head he returns it to Poppy.

'I'll have the crumble please with custard.'

'Thank you, about five minutes, okay?'

'Yep, fine.' He replies.

Nita slides round the table beside him and kissing his cheek says quietly.

'Just going to the little girl's room. I do love you ferryman!'

Turning in his seat he watches as she walks through the bar thinking how beautifully she moves; so elegant, she just seems to float effortlessly across the floor. He also notices one or two heads turn and follow her as she walks through the bar; he smiles to himself smugly thinking,

'You can look, but she's with me!'

Poppy emerges from the kitchen and walks to the table with Stephen's sweet.

'Thank you, that looks good.'

She smiles, turns and goes back to the kitchen passing Nita in the bar. Sliding back into her seat she cranes her neck across the table to inspect the bowl of crumble; reaching across the table she takes the spoon from his hand, dips it into the sweet and takes a small spoonful, blows on it to gently cool it then delicately slips into her mouth, savours it smiles and returns the spoon to his hand. Following her every move without saying a word he looks at the spoon back in his hand. He clears his throat.

'Huhmm, erm do you want some of your own or should I get another spoon…mmm?'

'No that was fine I just wanted to try it, you can have the rest.'

'Oh thank you… so kind, do you approve then?'

'Yes, very nice but so sweet.'

He takes his first spoonful, savours it and nods.

'That's really very good!'

He quite quickly consumes the remainder finally returning the spoon to the empty dish then realises Nita is watching him.

'What, have I got some on my chin?'

Shaking her head she giggles at him.

'No, I was just watching you devour that, you really enjoyed it didn't you?'

'Certainly did, now I want to go home and…'

'…. Make mad passionate love to me, yes?'

Hesitating momentarily he replies with a soft sigh.

'Ahhh, I was going to say go home crack the fire up watch a film until I doze off. I'm stuffed after that dinner but, okay we'll …'

'… No! we won't, you'll fall asleep and I won't get your full attention!'

Glancing towards her sheepishly he says.

'Sorry, come on sugar I'll get the bill and we'll head home shall we?'

Picking her bag up, she shuffles out from her seat playfully punching his arm as she stands beside him.

'You're a real charmer you… not!' she sighs, 'Ahh, where's the rampant passion gone in this relationship, we're becoming boring just an old couple set in our ways!'

Shaking her head she follows him to the end of the bar waiting to settle their bill. He suddenly jumps in response to Nita who's just subtly pinched his thigh then stroked the area affectionately. Staring at her, she smiles coyly turning her head away.

'Watch it you, you could get into trouble doing that!'

Returning his stare wide eyed she replies.

'Me… I haven't a clue what you're talking about!'

He hasn't time to answer her as the landlady Jean comes down the bar to them.

'Everything alright for you both?'

'Fine Jean thank you, we really enjoyed that, what's the damage then?'

Passing him the bill she says.

'Thirty-four, fifty with the drinks.'

He takes some money from his wallet and handing it to the landlady says.

'Put the change in the pot Jean, we really enjoyed that thank you.'

Nodding, Nita adds.

'Yes that was really very tasty. Listen if you hear from or see Mick tell him we were asking please; we'll try and catch up with him soon.'

'I will mi 'duck, like I said it feels really strange him not being here regularly, any way you two take care.'

Walking towards the door now they say, 'Goodbye.'

She smiles and responds, 'In a bit.'

Looking around as they drive away from the Duchess, Nita glances at her surroundings then at Stephen.

'Err, where are we going then?'

'A surprise!'

'Okay.'

Turning off the main road he drives further out into the countryside for another twenty minutes until they eventually stop. He reverses into a gateway on the edge of a copse of trees hiding them from any passing traffic. Stopping the engine and sitting back in his seat he looks at Nita who, to be fair is a little bewildered.

'You've not brought me out here to dispose of me have you?'

'Hmm,' he smirks, 'no my lovely lady but I am going to have my wicked way with you!'

Releasing her seat belt she half turns in her seat looking at him.

'You're going to have what? Half an hour ago we were going home and you were going to watch TV and fall asleep. Now you're going to ravish me… really!'

Releasing his belt he shuffles across his seat a little before reaching to embrace her.

'No… no Stephen, no!'

She protests and shies away from him further into the corner of her seat putting her hands on his shoulders to hold him back. Puckering his lips and blowing kisses towards her he continues to push himself nearer to her. Squashed into the corner of her seat now, still resisting his advances she says firmly.

'Stop it Stephen behave, act your age not your shoe size. You know you look really stupid.'

She says giggling but still holding him at bay; she feels herself weakening and begins to laugh at his childishness.

'Go on sugar, just one kiss… mmm… mmm.'

All resistance gone from her arms she submits to his advances until he lays on her chest raining wet, sloppy kisses on her cheeks and neck as she enfolds him in her arms, beating on his back playfully.

'Stop it… give up now! Stephen, enough!'

Still lying on her chest, gently snuggling into the nape of her neck.

'I absolutely adore you lady do you know that, I cannot believe there was someone out there who could make me so happy again. I love you sooo much!'

Holding him for some time, thinking about what he's just said, she kisses the top of his head.

'Do you remember that morning after our first night on the boat?' she says quietly.

'Mmm yes, you threw a right curved ball at me that morning.'

'Do you remember what I said when you eventually stopped and listened to me?'

'Something about your ordered life and it all going to mush.'

'Yes… in just two days you turned my life, my oh-so-organised world upside down and quite unexpectedly I found myself falling in love with you.' Kissing his head she continues, 'I found in you a really lovely man hiding away from the world. It felt like I'd awakened some kind of genie opening this bottle and you truly began to open up and let me in. The concern you'd shown your family since Suzanne died what fifteen, sixteen years ago. The deep love you have for Emma, the way you two show it to each other it's so special; I've watched you both, you just shut the world out when that happens, the bonus for me has been finding the hidden passion that was in there too. When we get passionate everything you do, your touch just sends shivers through me.'

She gently squeezes him. Responding he kisses the nape of her neck and caresses one of her breasts through her soft jumper; she squirms at his touch kissing the top of his head again.

'You know sometimes when I'm at work and we've been at it like rabbits the night before…' giggling now, 'I can still feel you holding me, touching me, you just possess me it makes me shiver; I'm sure Linda and Ruth can tell.'

Sliding his hand from her breast he slips it under the edge of her jumper and back up to caress her breast cupped in her bra. For a few minutes she allows him to caress her, sighing softly at his touch. Slipping a finger under the bra strap he tries to slide it from her shoulder to free her breast. She stops him, holding his hand firmly through the fabric.

'I know you want your wicked way with me but not here, take me home Ferryman!'

He pushes himself upright looks into her eyes the pupils are slightly dilated, leaning towards her, they kiss tenderly but with passion. Eventually separating they hold each other's gaze, repeating herself she says.

'Come on, take me home.'

Shuffling back onto his own seat he retraces their journey back to Portbridge, with a little difficulty this time as Nita is teasing him, alternating between resting her hand on his thigh gently stroking his leg and inner thigh and occasionally kissing his cheek and stroking his neck until they hit the main road.

Parking the car as near to their front door as he can, they walk to the front door. Opening it Nita slips past him; he closes the door turning to follow her into the house but he is immediately forcefully pushed back against the door as she presses herself against him kissing him passionately her tongue teasing his while her right hand caresses him until she feels him hard through his trousers. Breaking the kiss she growls at him, her voice husky with lust.

'Now you can ravish me as hard as you want!'

Taking his hand she sets off up the stairs pulling him behind her, dragging him to their bedroom. Spinning round she roughly pushes him in the chest and he falls across the bed, releasing her hair it cascades from her head down over her shoulders as she follows him onto the covers to half sit half lie across his chest, her lips once again back on his to continue another searching kiss. Struggling to breathe he fights to grasp and hold her arms to control her onslaught, gaining some control he pushes her upwards away from his chest and holds her there. In her eyes he sees the lust, the uncontrollable passion, staring at him breathing heavily and making little noises in her throat, he says.

'Whoa… slow down sugar.'

She continues fighting to release herself from his grasp, panting a reply.

'You started this Stephen… I want you now, I ache to feel you in me! I want you to just take me, make love to me… just screw me stupid… now Stephen!'

As she says this, she leans slightly to one side; seizing the opportunity he half turns to his right unseating her and rolls her onto her side to lie beside him. Releasing one arm he puts it around her waist drawing her closer, noses almost touching he says.

'I did not expect that!' he says kissing her, 'What brought this on lady?'

Putting her free arm round his shoulders, gently kissing him this time she replies.

'Even after seven years, you and sex still do the same to me now as you did then, I said to you earlier you make me shiver. Sometimes it's like the mini orgasms you give me when we make love they're like a drug and I'm your junkie… your sex junkie!'

Laughing, she slides back onto his chest and undoing his shirt kissing more of his chest as she exposes it, reaching the belt of his chino's she pull on it to release the clasp pulling the zip down then slipping her hand through the gap grasps and firmly caresses him. She is half sitting now and has her back to him, he slides his hands under the bottom of her jumper up until he reaches her bra quickly releasing the clasp then reaching to hold her breasts. She sighs at his touch, straightens herself a little revelling in the instant sensation he's giving her as he presses her nipples between his fingers.

'Ohh god…'

Pulling away from him she slips off the bed, reaches for the legs of his trousers and pulls them down his legs and off. Grasping at the waistband of his boxer shorts she drags those from him, discarding them onto the floor. Quickly she pulls her trousers off before climbing back to sit astride his thighs and continues to caress him. He slips his hands under her jumper and gently resumes moulding her breasts once more, dropping her head forward they kiss passionately.

'Enough… I want you now!' she says against his lips.

Shuffling into a more comfortable position and fumbling a little with their remaining clothing, she lowers herself onto his erection, sighing as she feels him deep inside her. Arms tightly wrapped around one another they stay perfectly still thrilling in the sensations this moment of intense intimacy they are feeling. He feels her muscles tensing and relaxing in spasms as he fills her inner self.

'Can you feel your muscles sugar? They keep squeezing me, it's like the sensation I get when you use your hands.'

Giggling she replies.

'Mmm… but I'm not actually doing anything, trust me if I move we're finished 'cause I'm going to cum soon!'

Dragging the end of this sentence out, her voice rises and she squeals a little, lifts herself ever so slightly from him then firmly sinks down onto him again immediately convulsing into spasms as she's wracked by her orgasm. It continues for some time as they hold onto each other. As her spasms subside he flips her onto her back further on the bed and begins to move driving himself deep into her sending her into another series of spasms.

'Ohh Stephen… oh my god…. don't stop… ahh yes, yes…'

Wrapping her legs tightly round his thighs locking him into her and throwing her arms round his shoulders she holds him tightly. Two final thrusts and he savours his own climax setting off Nita's third shattering orgasm in as many minutes.

Lying together they slowly recover their breathing, tears well up and she begins to cry uncontrollably, she feels his arms tighten around her reassuringly.

'Oh Stephen… I love you, I'm going to miss you, Stephen… Stephen!'

Chapter Two

'Nita, Nita wake up! Come on wake up, it's alright you're safe. Come on Nita wake up its Emma, you're having another nightmare but you're okay you're at home remember.'

Opening her eyes she stares at Emma for a few moments eyes wide, frightened. Reaching out she touches Emma's face seeking reassurance, she gently strokes it and begins crying again. Sitting beside her Emma lifts her into an embrace holding her until the tears and sobs diminish and she lies still.

'I had the dream again Em, I can't stand it when will it stop. when will I be able to sleep again without dreaming about him?'

'I know but it's alright it will get better it will. Remember the doctor said it could take some time but you will be able to sleep properly again. That's what the meds are for to help you through this bit.'

Close in their embrace, Nita says.

'What about you he was your dad, how are you managing Emma? You just seem so calm so sorted. I can't think, I can't do anything, I just want to curl up and… I don't know what I want anymore, how are you managing to function?'

Giving a little smile she replies.

'I have Angus and he's being an absolute brick, okay I keep falling apart then he just gets hold of me until I calm down. I'm so lucky Nita, plus there are the twins, I have to be strong for them. Mummy in bits upsets them they can't understand all this grief so I put the face on and carry on.'

She sits quietly still holding Nita lost in her own thoughts, until she says quietly.

'I guess this is how dad dealt with everything after mum died, he had to be strong for me even though he was a total wreck inside. He never really dealt with it you know, not until he met you; it was always there in the background but he put everyone else first. Perhaps that's how he got through it all.'

They hold each other neither of them speaking. They are both crying silently, tears flowing down their cheeks sharing their loss together, words are not needed just now. Emma shuffles into a more comfortable position still holding Nita in her arms and they lie there together.

A loud banging on the house door brings Emma awake and alert. She disentangles herself from the slumbering Nita quietly going down the stairs to open the door. Louise and Moira are standing there with bags and two dishes.

'We've been knocking for ages, is everything alright?'

'Sorry, it's been a bit tough this morning, come in,'

She steps aside to give the two girls room to enter, they go through to the kitchen and put the dishes and bags down.

'She's had the dream again, then when I got her calm we both fell asleep.'

Louise studies Emma for a few moments.

'What can we do? We're here to stay until the morning. What about you Em you must be absolutely shot.'

'I am to be honest the sedatives are only just touching her. She's calm for a while and sleeps, then as they wear a bit thin she keeps getting this recurring dream, it's so real to her. She's talking to him, you can hear her sometimes she's quite coherent, it's a bit scary really then the nightmare begins and she just loses it totally, twice last night she woke screaming his name.'

Louise goes to Emma embracing her.

'What do you want to do now we're here?'

'Honestly, I want to call Angus to come and get me, I want to go back to the hotel have a shower and see the twins.'

'Okay, let's make that happen me and Moira can take over here. When did she last eat? we've got food with us we were going to cook for you both but let's call Angus.'

'Do you want a tea Em?' Moira says.

'Please and a couple of tablets my heads pounding.'

'Okay, go… sit, Lou do you want to see if Nita's awake.'

'Yeah,'

She goes quietly upstairs. Sitting together in the lounge with their drinks as Louise returns, Emma asks.

'Awake or asleep?'

'Asleep, she seems quite peaceful.'

The three of them sit in silence sipping their drinks.

'Did you get hold of Angus?' Louise asks.

'Yeah, fifteen minutes or so.' Emma replies, 'Sure you'll be alright?'

The two girls nod, Moira says.

'It'll be like old times…well sort off.'

The three of them chuckle briefly, Emma looks at them.

'How's she going to cope tomorrow at the service? She's been like this for over two months now.'

Moira says thoughtfully.

'Maybe this could be the turning point for her,'

The two women glance at her waiting for her to continue.

'What I mean is, tomorrows service is like closure, it will be the final goodbye. Do you see what I'm trying to say?'

Louise and Moira look anxiously at Emma as she lets out a sob reaching for some tissues from the box on the coffee table and dabs her eyes, Moira says straight away defensively.

'Oh Em I'm sorry I didn't mean to upset you.'

Holding her hand up she says.

'No you're right, we get to say goodbye properly and start to pick our own lives up, rebuild and move on. Listen my mum is still here with me, in me,'

She gently beats her chest as she speaks.

'You never forget, but as time passes there comes a time when there is no need to re-visit that desolate place because you've begun to create a new history you know, memories that aren't so painful, but in here they remain. Mum has been here all my life,' she says her hand over her heart and her voice cracking with emotion, 'and dad is here now.' Smiling briefly she ends saying, 'they are together again after twenty years.'

A knock on the door stops the three of them from becoming more morose. Angus steps into the hall.

'Hello… car for Mrs Farquhar.'

He glances into the lounge as Emma gets to her feet and walks towards him and into his embrace.

'How's my girl?' he says,

'Not too good to be honest,' she replies, 'but this helps.' Hugging him tighter.

Louise and Moira look at each other.

'Do you know that soft highland tone is like warm chocolate,' Louise says, 'it just melts all over you, just need the marshmallows to finish it off.'

Moira nods in agreement as the four of them laugh, Emma says.

'I've never considered that before, but yes he's ever so softly spoken as are most people who come from the West and the islands.' She gives him a squeeze and smacks his bottom. 'Mind you he's got a right bark on him when he gets riled, you should hear him shouting when Scotland play England at rugby.'

'Hey, don't spoil it, I'm enjoying this.' Angus chips in. 'Right, you ready to go.' he says.

'I am,' glancing at the girls she says, 'Are you two sure you're going to be okay?'

Louise and Moira, having followed the couple into the hall smile.

'Go Emma… just you go, we've all lived together remember,' Louise says.

Moira nods. 'We'll make sure she's alright, go on go; have a shower and a rest and see those two yummy littlies. Give them a hug from us.'

The three women share a group hug briefly then Emma and Angus leave.

Chapter Three
9 Weeks Ago

Three heavy knocks on the door sounded above the playing CD, slipping off the settee Nita wormed her feet into her snug boots and padded to the door, opening it she grinned.

'You can always tell a coppers knock, there's just something about it.'

Standing on the doorstep she sees Alan Syms and her boss Ruth but she doesn't notice Alan's' sister behind him.

'I suppose you want a brew?'

Leaving the door open for them to follow, she turns walking to the kitchen. She'd only gone a few steps when she stopped turned looking at Alan and Ruth.

'Something's wrong… what's happened?'

'Yes, I'm sorry Nita.' Alan says, 'Look can we go and sit down?'

Nita changes direction leading them into the lounge, it was only then she sees Louise.

'Oh my god Alan what's happened, Lou why are you here?'

Taking her by an elbow Ruth says quietly.

'Do you want sit Nita?'

Ignoring her, she says firmly.

'No!' something's wrong, tell me!' staring at Alan.

'Nita, there's been an accident and I'm sorry but it's not good love.'

She inhales sharply catching her breath.

'Oh no what, who it's not Emma or the children is it… please no Alan. Stephen's still away.'

He shakes his head then glances at Ruth, she nods slightly.

'No, it's Stephen actually and I am so so sorry love, but it appears he's been killed!'

There's a pause… and then from Nita a sound that chills the room sending shivers through everyone there, an indescribable wail emanating from deep within her that becomes a howl of pain and emotion. She seemed to crumble as her legs gave way; had it not been for the fact that Ruth was still by her side she would have collapsed onto the floor. Louise quickly came to her other side to help Ruth lower her to the settee where she continued to sob and wail uncontrollably as she thrashed about on the settee. She was talking but no-one understood what she was saying. Louise tried to console her at the same time trying to calm her movements, Ruth called to a WPC who'd stayed in the hallway.

'Constable, see if you can find your way round the kitchen and make us some drinks please.'

'Sarge.' The officer replied.

Louise managed to get hold of Nita and was holding her firmly speaking to her quietly while she sobbed occasionally catching her breath, almost choking at times. They sat like this for some time until the WPC brought them some drinks. Much more in control and calmer Nita suddenly pushed herself away from Louise and dabbing her eyes said to Ruth and Alan.

'I need to call Emma… god how am I going to tell her and Mary and Richard. How… what do I say?'

She started to become emotional again and the low wail returned with the crying. She allowed Louise to embrace her as Ruth said stroking her leg.

'Nita you needn't worry about that, the Bristol guys have gone to tell Emma, you know it's standard procedure, you can call her later lovie.'

She nodded but stayed in Louise's embrace sobbing.

'Tell me what happened.'

'You don't need to know now lovie,' Ruth said, 'all that can come later.'

'No I want to know now then I can tell Emma what we know… please.'

'If you're sure.' Ruth replied.

Nita nodded, 'Yes… please.'

'Okay, so what we know so far has come from the German police. Stephen was travelling south to Strasbourg. Near Karlsruhe a north-bound truck crashed through the central reservation and collided with him and a number of cars, Stephen was one of a number of people who died I am so sorry Nita.'

No-one spoke for a while waiting as Nita tried to process what Ruth had just told her.

'Did they say if he suffered?'

Shaking her head Ruth replied quietly,

'They say he probably died instantly, the whole accident was caught on a motorway camera. They think the other driver possibly had a heart attack because of the way his truck suddenly swerved across his carriageway hitting some cars before crossing through the central reservation. We've requested the footage when they've completed their enquiries.'

Nita sat quietly again, going over in her mind questions then answering them herself. Standing up she said quietly.

'I need to call Emma.'

She wandered off into the kitchen but returned moments later looking at everyone.

'What was …' she just stood there before returning to the kitchen.

Louise got up and followed her, she was just standing at the breakfast bar.

'Nita,' she said, 'Nita what are you doing love?'

Looking over her shoulder Louise saw a completely vacant look in her eyes, taking her by the arm she said quietly.

'Come back into the living room and we'll see what we can do now, alright.'

She allowed herself to be led back to the lounge where she sat back on the settee. Ruth stood up.

'Right, we'll give you some space, if there's anything you need call the office or your brother, we'll do whatever we can. I'll stand her down for the moment on compassionate grounds, tell her not to worry. Right come on Alan let's leave them alone.'

'Boss,' he acknowledged then said to his sister as she followed them to the door.

'I'll come by tonight Sis okay.'

'Yeah we'll be okay, Moira's coming here so we'll all be together tonight, See you later.'

Returning to the front room she found Nita curled up on the settee in the foetal position staring into space and hugging a cushion. Sitting beside her she gently lifted her head resting it on her legs stroking her hair gently.

'I'm so sorry lovely this is just so unimaginably awful.'

She became aware Nita was shaking and in a few moments began to wail softly as before saying something she couldn't understand. After an hour of just sitting in the same position holding her, she sensed she'd become calm and when she moved slightly heard her moan. Realising she'd fallen asleep she shuffled herself and gradually slid out from under the slumbering form resting her head on a cushion. Standing, she stretched to ease her muscles after sitting in the one position for so long. Taking her mobile she walked into the kitchen switched the kettle on and called Moira, she answered immediately.

'Hey, how are things, how's Nita coping with this dreadful news?'

'Not sure,' Louise replied, 'she's behaving oddly and I haven't a clue what she's saying, it must be in Urdu or something. Listen pick supper up on your way over will you, just choose something we all like I'm not sure Nita will want much to eat.'

'Okay will do, do you want anything from home?'

'Oh yes, night stuff and a change of undies please and my cosmetic bag from the bathroom.'

'Right see you just after six, bye.'

'Yeah bye.'

Louise made herself a drink and sat at the breakfast bar trying to anticipate what the next hours and days were going to be like. She jumped, shocked by the sound of the telephone ringing, searching for it she went into the lounge to see Nita holding the handset, she heard her sob as she said.

'I don't know what to say, I can't take it in just now. I'm still thinking he's going to come home next week.'

She listened to the unknown caller for a while then asked.

'How's Emma, who's helping with the twins, do you want me to come down Angus. Has anyone spoken to Mary and Richard do you know?'

They must have said no because she said.

'You just have to call and I'll be there in the day. Don't struggle Angus I'm here I'll help okay!'

Whatever was said next brought back the choking tears again and unable to speak she looked at Louise holding the handset out to her; taking it she said.

'Hi Angus its Louise I'm not sure what you just said but she can't speak just now.'

She listened as he related his conversation and the possibility she'd miss-heard his answer regarding Richard and Mary, she responded saying.

'Right, I understand I'll tell her when she's calm again, Moira and I are staying with her tonight for definite, we'll see how tomorrow pans out and decide what to do then. The police have offered as much help as they can. Angus give Emma our love, we are so deeply sorry. We'll speak later okay, bye.'

Replacing the handset she turned her attention to Nita who'd returned to the settee and curled up again sobbing. She went and sat with her just so she could feel the comfort of someone's arms around her. When she spoke to her there was no response, it seemed she'd completely withdrawn become introvert and that worried her. They were still in this position when Moira arrived laden with their dinner and bags from the house for the overnight stay. Putting everything down in the hallway and kitchen she eventually came into the lounge and sat down.

'How are we, is there any change?'

Louise shook her head.

'No, she's been like this since Alan and the sergeant left. Angus called and she spoke to him briefly and since then nothing. She cries from time to time and is talking a lot but I don't understand what she's saying, I'm really worried Moira.'

Moira thought for a while.

'Let's get our stuff sorted first and eat then see how she is, I'll get the food out.'

Louise nodded and said to Nita.

'Moira's brought dinner in should we eat then talk about how we can help you?'

'I don't want anything I'm not hungry but you two eat.'

'Nita you've got to eat sweetie.'

She shook her head, 'No, I'm alright honestly.'

Louise moved and Nita lifted her head to allow her to stand up then lay back in the foetal position again hugging the cushion. The two girlfriends sat at the bar in the kitchen and ate the Chinese meal Moira had brought with her while Louise brought her up to date on what they knew of Stephen's accident. Nita never moved occasionally bursting into tears and talking. Later in the evening Alan Syms turned up to see how everyone was coping and seeing Nita on the settee was, like the others, concerned, as he was leaving he said.

'Call me in the morning and let me know how the night has gone, if she's much the same I'll see if the boss can get our police Doc to see her, she might need some help you know.'

'Yeah, okay, speak then. Take care going home love.'

Louise said as she gave him a hug.

The girls set about encouraging Nita to try and eat something before going to bed. She still refused the food but they did manage to get her to take a shower then go to bed. Louise and Moira shared the bed in the spare room. In the early hours of the morning they were woken by Nita wailing again and shouting out Stephen's name. They rushed to her room to find her sitting up pressed against the headboard of the bed tears streaming down her face, eyes wide open saying repeatedly.

'Stephen, I love you… so much… I'm going to miss you, Stephen… Stephen.'

Both girls climbed onto the bed, Louise taking her in her arms even though Nita tried to push her away; Moira said quickly.

'She's not awake Lou, she's still in the dream.'

'Nita… Nita wake up love you're dreaming.' Louise said firmly.

'No, no he was here, I was talking to him we'd just made love… he was here!'

'No Nita, I'm so sorry love he wasn't here, you were dreaming.'

She suddenly threw herself away from Louise across the bed wailing uncontrollably saying something neither of them could understand. They tried to gather her up to restrain and console her but she just kept thrashing around and crying out. For more than an hour they tried to calm her.

No one managed much sleep after this but the girls decided Moira should try and get some rest as she had to be at her school in the morning, whereas Louise would phone her office and take a bit of leave. In the morning Nita slept peacefully allowing Louise and Moira time to shower and face the day, jaded but a little refreshed. After breakfast Moira left to travel to her school, Louise called Alan a short time later explaining last night's events and asked if he could get the police doctor to come over.

It was mid-morning when there was a knock on the door, Louise opened it to see Ruth, Nita's Inspector and a gentleman she took to be the doctor. Ruth smiled and introduced Doctor Choudhry. They all went into the lounge where Louise took them through last night's events and how things had gone so far today.

'Where is Nita now?' the doctor asked.

'She's still in bed, she's been drinking a little but we haven't been able to get here to eat anything since you were all here yesterday.' she said glancing at Ruth.

'Am I alright to go up and see her?' the doctor said, 'I think you'd better come with me, we don't want to agitate her any more by suddenly seeing a strange face appear in her bedroom.'

The three of them laughed at the thought of him appearing in the bedroom and sending Nita into a moment of hysteria. After talking to her and running some simple health checks he administered a sedative and they all returned to the lounge.

'Okay, Nita is showing all the signs of deep emotional trauma. This isn't going to go away without help, a lot depends on how she deals with it herself initially, I feel she's going to need a course of anti-depressants though. I've given her mild sedative to help her rest and sleep, otherwise she's going to end up in hospital. Ideally she needs someone here with her all the time just now, how much family support can she rely on?'

Both the doctor and Ruth looked at Louise for an answer, she shrugged.

'Well Moira and I can stay for a while, I've taken leave this week but until we've spoken to the family, I don't know.'

Taking a card from his pocket he wrote a number on it, handing it to her.

'My mobile and landline number,' he said, 'call anytime, I'll come over.'

'Louise keep us in the loop please,' Ruth said, 'I'm sure Alan will help if he can but so can we, don't forget.'

'I will,' she replied, 'I'll call the family when you've left. We'll try and sort out some sort of a support thing, I'll let you know.' She glanced at Ruth.

As soon as they'd left Louise went to see that Nita was comfortable. Seeing the sedative was still being effective she returned to the lounge and decided to call Richard and Mary to sort out what was the best course of action to support Nita immediately and look at the long term. It was a sombre call but at the end of it they decided between them that Richard would come to Portbridge and Mary would go to Bristol to help Angus with Emma and the twins.

Late afternoon the following day Louise answered a knock on the door to see Richard standing on the pavement, he grinned.

'Reinforcements, the cavalry have arrived!'

Louise replied, 'Hello, good to see you, how was the trip?'

'Oh, no problems you know.' he said as he followed here to the lounge. 'How's Nita?'

Louise looked at him and began to up-date him on how things had developed since yesterday, he listened taking everything in she said.

'Is she eating and drinking?'

'Hmm, only picking at her food but, yes she's drinking, the biggest problem is the nightmare she keeps having. Last night and the previous one too, she wakes almost hysterical calling his name and throwing herself about, it gets quite physical trying to calm her. Tonight will be the second one using the sedatives the police Doc prescribed. She's been calmer generally today with the tablets so we're hoping tonight might be better too. Do you know how Emma's coping?'

'Not well understandably, Angus is struggling a little with her and the twins but Mary should be there about now and Iain and Elspeth are hoping to be there tomorrow, Mary's going to come here then and we'll plan something more long term with you and Moira.'

Later that afternoon Nita was lying peacefully in bed, Louise had taken her some refreshment up and told her Richard was here. He went up and sat with her for some time talking quietly to her. When he came downstairs he said to Louise.

'She's hungry but doesn't know what she wants. I've made a few suggestions and we've settled on a fish from the chippie. Will you two be okay with that?'

Louise shrugged and replied.

'Absolutely, anything to get her to eating again. I'll message Moira to collect them on the way home.'

'Good, I've suggested she comes down later and has it with us. We need to get her to move around, change rooms to help break up the pattern in her head that set's off the nightmares.

Louise grinned at Richard.

'Your good at this aren't you, we could have done with you here that first night.'

He shook his head.

'No… no that was pure shock, no-one could have done anything with her then just sedate her.'

Just before Moira was expected home they managed to encourage Nita to take a shower and come down and sit with them. There wasn't much conversation, the long silences filled by the chatter from the television; Nita just sat embracing a cushion staring into oblivion. Once their supper arrived it was shared out and they all sat in the lounge eating. They were all relieved to see her eat all her fish and the few chips they each offered.

Chapter Four

Final Closure.

Although the day is cool and grey it is fine and expected to remain so for most of the day. Most of Stephens's family have gathered at the terraced house during the morning ready to leave for the Parish church in the centre of Portbridge for the memorial service at one thirty. Drinks, snacks and nibbles have been available all morning for those feeling in need of some sustenance although the atmosphere in the house is understandably quiet and sombre. Periodically throughout the morning Nita has continued to dissolve into tears. Everyone has taken time to support her encouraging her to get ready. Emma and the girls have administered the tablets supplied by the police doctor to help her remain calm and alleviate the anxiety of the coming service. There is a firm knock on the door which when opened reveals Thomas Sugden the undertaker dressed in a full morning suit, Angus beckons him into the house.

'Morning, I think we're ready, well as ready… you know!'

Angus comments. Thomas Sugden nods.

'We've one car here, the second has gone to the hotel for Mr Grace, the grandparents and the children; they are going straight to the Duchess.

Angus nods then asks.

'It's coming to the church then to transport the main party back to the Duchess after the service?'

'Yes that's right.'

Emma emerges from the lounge followed by Mary and Richard, Thomas acknowledges them as they hear Nita come down the stairs.

'I need some water I'm parched.' she says standing on the bottom step.

'I'll get it.'

Mary says touching her arm, moments later she hands her the drink. Glancing at everyone she says.

'Will I do?'

She's wearing the same vibrant blue trousers she wore the first evening she and Stephen had dinner together at the Duchess and the embroidered chemise. She's put her hair up which shows off her beautiful neck. Angus is the first to answer as he holds his hand out to see her down the last step.

'Oh yes, you look amazing.'

His comment prompts a responsive prod from Emma.

'Hey, just remember you're with me!'

Everyone smiles briefly, Richard edges his way towards the door.

'Come on folks, let's get this show on the road should we?'

He nods to Thomas Sugden who turns and opening the door steps onto the street. He opens the door of the black Limousine, the driver does the same on the other side. Nita looks around the street noticing some of their neighbours who have come out to watch.

In the centre of town the organ at the Parish church quietly plays a selection of incidental music as people arrive for the service picking up an order of service at the entrance as they make their way into the church. By the time the clock chimes the quarter hour it is almost full everyone quietly chatting to friends or making introductions to strangers sitting with them. It's evident everyone has responded to the request that the service is a celebration of Stephen's colourful life and taken heed of the light and bright dress code. Bright dresses are scattered around the church amongst a few Hawaiian shirts. The tower clock chimes the half-hour and as the last of the chimes fade away the Limousine bringing the family draws up at the gates to the church. Louise and Moira are standing with the vicar on the path to the church. With everybody out of the car the girls embrace Nita then the family. The vicar greets the group.

'Good afternoon Nita, hello everyone welcome, are you ready to begin Nita?' He adds straight away, 'It will be alright you know, listening to some of the people here it appears you and Stephen were part of one very large family and they are waiting to share this service with you.'

She smiles at him but her eyes are vacant, Louise links her arm on one side, Moira does the same on the other. Speaking quietly Emma says.

'Have we all got tissues?'

After a moment fumbling and passing around of paper hankies, Richard and Angus nod to the vicar. They set off to walk into the church, at the door they pause for a moment until the organ begins to play a piece of music chosen by Nita and the family. Like a rolling wave the congregation stand as the family move up the aisle; Thomas Sugden escorts them to the front three pews where they sit as the music finishes; from the choir steps the vicar turns to look at a sea of faces.

'Hello and welcome to St Oswald's we are here today to remember Stephen and to give thanks celebrating his life, to many of you he was known only by his CB name 'Ferryman', I'm told it's called a handle, to others he was just Stephen. My name is Jonathan and I'm the vicar here at St Oswald's, I have to confess I never had the opportunity to meet Stephen and until ten days ago had not met Nita or Emma, but I am indebted them and close members of the family for allowing me to get to know them and immensely privileged to have got to know something of Stephen the person, his life, work and family. We begin this service with a hymn chosen by Emma it was one she often sang with her dad at school services.'

After the hymn had finished, Jonathan invited Emma to come and speak about Stephen and her memories through the years. Angus accompanied her to the pulpit where she spoke of the special relationship with her dad; how after eight years on his own after her mum had died he'd met Nita and how for them, for her and her grandparents Richard and Mary and Grandpa Harold, she'd at last got her real dad back in her life again. Towards the end of her recollections, when she recalled more recent times with Angus and the twins, how much he'd loved them and doted over them she became a little emotional; Angus gently slipped his arm round her waist for support.

Once back in their seats, Jonathan shared a reading from the scriptures about death and everlasting life before speaking to everyone on the behalf of Nita and the family. For the next ten minutes, he spoke of Stephen and some of the antics he got up to that had the congregation frequently chuckling, especially when relating sailing experiences and holidays with the family. He spent time recalling Stephen's compassionate side, especially if he saw an injustice being done or met someone who was feeling threatened, victimised, or suffering emotionally. How he'd go out of his way to find them the help they needed. Jonathan went on to say how Stephen himself had experienced some hard times first-hand especially when Suzanne became ill and passed away. This left him with a much-traumatised little girl to care for while at the same time coping with his own grief. How the purchase of *Finbar ll* gave him an out for himself and all the family to escape the problems and tribulations of work, school and college, giving them a chance to relax and see something of Britain and Europe from a different perspective visiting little islands and secluded bays. He concluded his eulogy by summing up Stephen's calmness and gentle disposition in any crisis which showed him to be a man with a big heart and an even bigger love for his family especially Nita and Emma and that his presence in this life was going to be missed by those he loved and who he'd met over the years. The organist played a short piece of music that meant a lot to Stephen allowing everyone to reflect on the vicars and Emma's words.

After a series of prayers for Stephen's repose and the family and the final committal there followed a final hymn. Just before he gave a blessing he addressed the congregation once more.

'The family have asked me to extend an invitation to you all to join them at the Duchess for drinks and refreshments and to share your memories of your friendships with Stephen with the family. Before I say the grace and give the blessing I'd like to read you something which Stephen wrote some years ago that Nita wanted me to share with you. Now you Knights of the road will understand this instantly, but I'd ask you to translate these words to those around you who may not understand its meaning, it reads.

Breaker 1-9 for a copy, this is the Ferryman, heads up guys, keep the shiny side up and the dirty side down, keep the pedal to the metal. Be safe, keep on trucking, I'll see you on the flip side. This is the Ferryman down on the side and out.'

There was silence through the church, broken only by a few quiet sobs here and there, until somewhere amid the congregation someone began to clap. It was taken up by others until the whole church resounded to loud applause that lasted for minutes. Eventually when peace settled again, Jonathan gave the peace and shared the blessing before the organist played a final piece of music.

Thomas Sugden came to Nita and the family to escort them from the church. As they walked back up the aisle Nita noticed some familiar faces in the congregation, among them some uniforms too. She suddenly saw her sister and a friend at the back of the church, reaching out she took her sisters hand and pulled her to walk out with them. Outside both Limousines were parked at the end of the path. She hugged her sister.

'Thank you!' she said, they hugged again. 'Will you come to the Duchess?'

Her sister shook her head.

'No I can't, you understand I just wanted to tell you how heartbroken I am for you. Baba asked me to say how sorry he is too he liked Stephen, he respected him for coming to our house that Christmas and facing the family, that can't have been easy for him. He's asked for prayers at the mosque that's really something you know. Do you think you can come and visit sometime; will you forgive us it's been seven years, I'd like to see you back in the family, will you think about it… please?'

As they hugged again Nita said softly, 'I'll think about it, yes.'

Her sister stepped away and they continued towards the waiting cars where she was surprised to see officers on duty plus two motorcycle outriders at the front and a traffic car at the rear. A little stunned she turned to seek out Ruth her Inspector in the crowd gathering outside the church. Her eyes fell on her previous boss, Detective Superintendent Allen, he held her gaze for a moment then nodded slightly, then saw Ruth by his side; she simply smiled. Soon both cars were ready to move and were led away by the two police bikes who stopped the traffic near the church until the two limousines were on their way to the Duchess. A short time into the journey Angus squeezed Emma's thigh, she looked at him.

'Is this how the Royal family feel do you think?'

One of the two bikes sped past their car up to the next intersection. Shrugging her shoulders she replied.

'I guess they're used to it really.'

Richard, sitting behind them commented.

'I've been stopped by them a few times back in the day.'

Emma glances at Angus grinning.

'You have too haven't you, hhmm?'

He shrugs, 'Yeah okay.' giving her a chased look.

As the convoy drove through town Nita notices some people watch its progress.

'I wonder what they're thinking.'

Everybody looked around at the street and pavement for a few moments before she added.

'That was a really nice service considering the vicar didn't know any of us.'

'It was and so many people there,' Richard added, 'just goes to show how others knew Stephen in different ways, you have to ask yourself how many others lives he touched over the years.'

Reaching forward Mary strokes Emma's shoulder.

'You did brilliantly Em, what you said about dad was just lovely well done.'

'Thanks nan but it was Angus who got me through it.' She kisses his cheek, saying softly, 'thank you.'

He smiles, 'you're welcome my love.'

The little convoy and escort finally come to a stop at the front steps of the Duchess. Thomas Sugden and the driver get out opening the doors for the family to gather on the pavement with those from the second car. As they move towards the steps into the Duchess, Nita briefly seeks out Thomas and shaking his hand says.

'I can't thank you enough for today, you've made it manageable for me, will you thank the others please.'

Nodding he replies.

'Certainly, it has been a privilege to have been able to help you through this painful time, please accept my personal condolences. I've learned quite a bit about Stephen and his passion and compassion for his fellow man. If you need anything else, any advice regarding documents or form filling don't hesitate to call my office, I'd be more than happy to help you through that jungle.'

They both smile, Nita turns to re-join the family when spots a police sergeant standing beside the traffic car at the back of the convoy, touching Emma and Angus's arms briefly, she says.

'Just give me a minute,'

Turning she walks towards the officer, he smiles at her as she gets nearer to him and removes his hat.

'Thanks for this Sam, a bit of a surprise mind but thank you.'

'It was the Super's idea he cleared it with our Inspector. Some of us got know Stephen through you and what he got involved in, the important thing is Nita, we are all so sorry!'

She touches his arm, squeezing it gently.

'Thank you, will you say thanks to the lads here please, he'd have loved the escort you know!'

Replacing his hat he salutes her.

'Yeah no probs we'll get off now. You take care Nita we'll see you back soon.'

She walks back to the family waiting on the steps to the pub, raising an arm to the two bikers at the front of the cars, they acknowledge her then proceed to follow the traffic car away into Portbridge.

Together they go up half dozen steps and through the original ornate Victorian entrance into the hallway of the Duchess, Nita notices a sandwich board by the door.

The Duchess will be closed
Until 7pm this evening
For a private party.

She smiles, more to herself than the others, thanking Jean in her head. Emma notices the smile and takes her arm giving it a gently squeeze.

'Well it was sort of your local wasn't it?'

Nita glances at her briefly nodding, 'Mmmm.'

Before they come into everyone's view in the bar they hear animated chatter and laughter. Nita stands still looking at Emma, Angus and the others, they are suddenly aware of the pain that she's tried to hide through the day and service.

'I don't think I can do this, it's too much. I don't want to be here, I'm sorry I want to go home… please!'

Emma and Angus each take an arm and lead her back to an antique chair that sits beside an ornate hat stand at the bottom of the stairs. Mary comes and crouches by her side as Emma disappears to the bar returning quickly with a glass of water. Taking two tablets from a bottle in her handbag she passes them and the glass to Mary who quietly talks to Nita, encouraging her to take the tablets. They stay here for some time while Mary talks to Nita, stroking her hand occasionally and embracing her. She nods from time to time at what Mary is saying to her, eventually Mary stands. Nita takes a deep breath and gets up, the two women embrace and Nita looks around, smiles briefly but with tears in her eyes and say's.

'I'm okay now, sorry just had a moment,' looking directly at Emma, 'you know one of those moments?'

Grinning Emma nods.

'Oh yes, they're special moments those!'

Holding hands with Mary and Emma they all walk into the bar. A wave of silence spreads across the room as those gathered become aware of Nita and the family's arrival. In complete silence Nita looks at the family then at everyone else and grins.

'I don't think I've ever had this effect on so many people at one time before. Hhmm, do you think if I leave you'll all begin chattering again?'

A ripple of laughter runs around the room and the general atmosphere lifts as people relax and the conversation volume gradually increases once more. Jean comes from behind the bar to stand beside her slipping her arm round her waist.

'Hello duck are you alright now you had a little wobble earlier; how was the service?'

As she speaks she gently propels her through the bar towards the dining room, Nita reply's.

'I'm fine Jean thanks,' smiling briefly, 'if I keep taking the tablets I can cope. Yes it was a lovely service, just so many people there I hardly recognised any of them.'

Giving her arm a squeeze Jean says.

'Just goes to show what a special man he was to so many people. Anyway you'll never guess who's appeared!'

She looks at Jean, 'Go on...'

The landlady searches the faces and heads in the bar looking for someone but before she sees who she wants, someone behind them says.

'Afternoon detective.'

Jean grins as Nita spins around.

'MICK,' she exclaims, 'oh my god, it's you, you're here! How are you, oh it's so good to see you.' she puts her arms around him giving him a hug.

'Me, oh I'm all right, eey I was so sorry to hear about Stephen, a real gent that one, posh name but no edge on him he were a good'n, hard to find many like him these days.'

Stepping back a pace she strokes his shoulder saying very softly.

'Thank you,' adding, 'is it me or have you lost some weight? Listen I need to circulate and say hello to everyone, can we catch up later is that okay?'

He nods, 'You know where to find me, I'll be at that end of the bar and yes about 3 stone,' he chuckles, 'I'm wearing stuff I've had for more than 10 years.' He pulls on the waistband of his trousers to show how loose they are and grins.

'We'll have a catch up later detective.'

Turning he makes his way back through the mass of bodies around the bar, Nita turns back to Jean, who's still smiling says.

'He just walked through the door about an hour ago just as though he'd never been away, you could have knocked me over with a feather. Now first, drinks at the bar are sorted, the girls know about the family's drinks.' Gesturing with her arm she says, 'I hope you're happy with the spread, we pulled all the stops out.'

Nita stands at the entrance to the dining room and stares.

'Jean there's so much it looks fabulous thank you, are you sure you're covered for all this?'

'Sure mi' duck don't worry I called in a couple of favours, this one is special. Now do you want a drink?'

'Oh please, a spritzer but with lemonade thanks. I'm going to find the family and see if they're alright.

Jean say's as sets off back to the bar.

'I've reserved the window bay for you all, there are two tables set so you should all have enough room.'

Nita follows her back towards the bar, then turns to weave her way towards the bay window acknowledging some of the people she recognises until she stands by the tables where the family are. Harold and Sylvie are tucked in one corner next to the twin's other grandparents Iain and Elspeth. Emma, reunited with Rory and Elizabeth is listening to their animated chatter, Angus and his twin Stewart are somewhere by the bar getting drinks for everyone. The bar bell chimes out and the bar falls silent. Nita hears Angus announce that food is ready from the dining room and everyone should help themselves. A ragged cheer goes up and the chatter begins again as people move to the dining room. Nita stands by the table watching the twins for a while until Emma whispers something in Elizabeth's ear, the little girl looks up and around the room until her eyes fall on Nita.

'Nani,' she squeals, 'Nani,' setting off round the table, pushing past the assorted knees and legs of the family, until free of the obstacle course runs straight into Nita's arms. Rory responds pretty much the same way when he sees Nita. She stands now with a child in each arm as they hug and kiss her neck and cheeks. Turning her head from one side to the other trying to breathe through this onslaught, she responds with the odd kiss strategically placed on the children. Those guests closest to the table turn and watch laughing and sighing at the loving sight. Through the crowd Angus and Stewart return with the drinks order placing them on the tables. Angus plucks Rory from Nita as Stewart takes Elizabeth, Angus says.

'Come on you two give Nani a break she needs a drink and to go and say hello to all these friends who've come to remember Gramps; who would like a crisp hmmm?'

He passes two packets of crisps to Harold and Sylvie, the twins follow the packets standing beside the adults until they open them.

Nita turns to Emma. 'How have they been?'

'Yeah, everyone says they've been good, spoiled rotten apparently by Jean and the girls. I don't think they'll be very hungry.'

Nita half sits beside Harold taking his hand in hers looking into his eyes, they are bright but she sees sadness in them, he looks tired and drained, she kisses his cheek softly.

'How are you holding up? It was a lovely service, all these people were there and more. He meant a lot to so many people Harold, you should be proud of him.'

His eyes fill with tears as he tries to reply but the words fail to come. Putting her arms around him she says gently.

'I'm so sorry Harold, it will get better with time honestly it will.'

Struggling, he replies this time, his voice cracking with emotion.

'It's so hard love, first my Betty then Suzanne and now my boy. It's killing me Nita what's it doing to our Emma, both her mum and dad gone! I honestly don't know how you're managing love, he was a great lad and you two were just so good together.'

He becomes quiet resting in Nita's embrace, close to his ear she says quietly.

'Don't get me started Harold because if I do I'll not stop I just want to hide away, I can't see tomorrow let alone the future!'

'Eee lass I'm sorry.'

Separating they look into each other's eyes as Nita says.

'There's food Harold, if you or Sylvie want anything send one of the boys, yes?'

'Aye I will.'

Disengaging herself from their embrace she stands.

'I'm going to say hello to some of these people, back soon.'

She smiles at Sylvie briefly and picking up her drink, says to them all.

'Go and get some food, there's loads.' Shuffling past Angus she adds, 'See to Harold and Sylvie will you?'

He nods and she touches his shoulder as she begins to make her way across the bar to the first group of people she wants to speak to, her work colleagues; Ruth takes her hand as she stands by them.

'I suppose you're sick of folk asking lovie but, how are you doing?'

She giggles momentarily and rolls her eyes a little.

'To be honest it's just going over my head at the moment.' She turns to Superintendent Allen, 'Thank you for today sir unexpected but so thoughtful.'

With a wry smile he replies.

'Not a problem, there were murmurings from some of the sections who's paths he'd crossed who thought of him as an honorary copper so the Inspector and I got our heads together and came up with the plan.'

'Well thank you it meant a lot, he would have loved it.'

Ruth chips in.

'He was a bit of a loose cannon mind wouldn't you say, if he thought something was off he was like a terrier with a rag until either he sorted it or we did?'

The whole group laughed.

'That said,' the Super added, 'he did help us out a few times, we certainly cleared some cases.'

'Listen,' Nita said, 'please go and get so food okay, I need to say some hellos'. I'll try and catch you later.'

She turned to circulate among other little groups of people, Linda reached out and held her arm firmly.

'Listen my lovely lady don't be a bloody hero and say you're alright! You've got my number I couldn't care a shit what time of day or night it is, if you're down you call… understand!'

Nita looked at the hand on her arm then into her eyes, she smiled very briefly.

'I will, thank you.'

Linda continued holding her arm, only a little more firmly and said a little more forcefully.

'I mean it Nita, you call me!'

She glanced at her again and nodded letting her hand slide affectionately across Linda's shoulder.

Across the room she saw Christine the transport manager from the depot. She was standing among a group of men, some Nita recognised as other drivers Stephen worked alongside, Chris smiles at her as she makes her way across to them.

'Hi, can I just say you look beautiful I love what you're wearing, it can't have been easy for any of you today. He would have been so proud of Emma what she said was so true of the person he was. The boss sends his condolences and apologies, he's stayed at the depot manning the phones as so many of us, the drivers, wanted to be here to show their support and love for you all.'

Taking an envelope from her bag she hands it to her.

'There's a card everyone has signed and a note from the boss for you.'

Taking the envelope from Christine she says.

'Thank you I'll look at it later, there have been so many cards and notes from people I haven't a clue who they are but they were people he knew through you and work or before we got together. I'll get around to reading them when things settle down a bit, thank you.'

Looking at the group around her she says.

'Please all of you go and eat, there's food in the dining room just help yourselves.'

Christine touches her arm.

'I know you want to circulate but there's someone in particular who wants to meet you properly. You have met before but you weren't really aware he was there.'

Nita looks at her quizzically as she gently pulls a tall blond man from the group.

'Nita this is Erik, Erik Van Dryke, you sort of met a few years ago.'

Erik holds his hand out and she takes it, when he spoke she clearly heard his strong Dutch accent.

'Ya acht yara sorry, eight years ago, ve crash on der auto route, the ring road here at Portbridge. I think I killed you and Stephens kinder…. er daughter.'

Nita grins at him, 'Yes, I only know what people have told me about that night. I saw the pictures the traffic officers took and I can understand how you thought we might have both died, I think Emma and I need to thank you actually. My colleagues tell me that we were so lucky, if you hadn't had your wits about you and been so alert it could have ended badly for us, so thank you.'

'Oh ya for sure, I thank mine Gott that you both got out safely. I would have… err… problem,' Erik searched for the word, 'difficult… ya… in mine life if you did not go free er escape ya?'

She touches his arm, 'Well we did Erik thanks to you. Now please go and get some food with the others and take care out there, yes!'

Almost standing to attention he gives a kind of bow, 'Danke, thank you.'

Chris turns to Nita as Erik follows the other drivers to the dining room.

'He was one of many drivers who called the office when the news of the accident hit the media. Apparently he often criss-crossed to and from Holland with Stephen, there are three drivers here from Germany and one from France. It's strange isn't it, a totally different world we really know nothing about. Their lives are centred on this little seven by ten world for days and weeks sometimes, we just take it for granted so long as they make the deliveries. Did you know some of them prefer their cabs to being at home with their wives, they can't wait to go again.'

Nita thought about what Chris had just said for a few moments then says.

'I've never seen it like that before but you're right, Stephens head was somewhere else the night before he was away. Even when he got onto the home runs, in the morning he was like a robot sorting stuff out.' She stops and gasps, 'Even this last time.' She choked a little in her throat as she finished the sentence, Christine reached to hold her arm.

'I'm so sorry Nita, I do know how hard it is. Even after all these years since my Owen passed it still catches me out from time to time. Listen, if you are struggling and just want to talk, call the depot and I'll come to you.'

'Thank you Chris that's comforting.'

'Nita, it's not a hollow promise I do know what it's like and I will come and meet you. We all loved him you know, he was one of the good ones, honestly.'

Nita took a breath to fight back the tears then looking at Christine said.

'Thank you, look go and get some food okay.'

She nods, turns and makes her way through the throng of people. Nita turned to go and see how the family were getting on but stops beside a couple sitting at one of the bar tables, she takes a double take and says.

'Shamir?

The woman grins, getting to her feet, they embrace hugging each other.

'I don't believe it, Shamir! I hardly recognised you, you look so different all grown up now.'

'I'm very well, we are very well,' she turns to look at the man with her.

'David,' Nita said, 'my you look a whole lot better than the last time I saw you.'

She guides Shamir back to her seat again and sits with them as David reply's.

'Yeah I'm good thanks Miss Patel.'

Nita holds her hand up, 'Oh call me Nita for god's sake, Miss Patel makes me sound like an old maid.'

Glancing at the pair she asks, 'So has everything worked out for you two?'

Shamir grins glancing at David.

'It has yes,' showing Nita her left hand and the rings on her finger. 'We married nearly five years ago, we have a two-and-a-half-year-old son Stephen and we're having another baby in February.'

Nita claps her hands excitedly.

'How wonderful, I'm so happy for you both and you called your son Stephen.'

David says, 'Yes we owed so much to him for what he did that day and how much he suffered in the end for getting involved.'

He paused, looked at Shamir then says.

'We saw the news on television, we are so sorry Nita.'

He hesitated, she saw Shamir's hand rest gently on his thigh, quietly and emotionally he adds.

'I'm sorry I can't find the words, we… we are just so sorry.'

Nita looked at them both.

'Thank you and thank you for coming today it does mean a lot, really. So tell me what you are both doing now, are you still in the Midlands?'

Shamir answered, 'No, David got a job at a private school near Lincoln to teach IT that was almost five years ago. I applied for a post with a Historical research organisation based at the Cathedral and got that post six months later. It's good because after having Stephen I've been able to work from home so could manage the baby stuff and still get on with my job; they've been very good about it.'

'And you David,' Nita asked, 'are you alright now, no lasting problems?'

'I am thank you, it took some time before I felt confident enough to go back into main-stream work. I had a short-term memory problem for a while but once that settled down and with this lady's help I made it, we made it. The job at the school was the cherry on the cake really because it's kind of an insular existence. I feel safe there and can give it a hundred percent.'

Nita grinned at them both.

'And your families, how are things there?'

She saw them exchange a quick glance.

'Mmmm, problems then?' Nita asks.

Shamir shrugged, 'Yeah you could say that, David's family are fine they've been so good ever since we were attacked and when we got married they were great, then when Stephen came along well we'd never see him if they had their way. My family that's a different story; basically they've disowned me because of the dishonour thing. Remember that's what kicked it all off, I don't think they'll ever forgive me plus the fact that my brother and cousin served time.'

'Do you think there'll ever be any chance of a reconciliation?' Nita says.

Shamir shakes her head, 'Sadly no, you know how traditional many families are, and David and I are definitely not on the Christmas list.' She glanced at David again and they both laughed briefly, 'We laugh about it now, how pointless it is to carry on the dislike even after all this time.'

She sighed, it sounded like a sigh of resignation to Nita, then said.

'Their loss in the end, but I do get up-set sometimes, we keep trying to offer the olive branch…'

She shrugs again, David reached across stroking her shoulder sympathetically, Nita reached for her hand giving it a squeeze.

'Not easy Shamir I'm sorry, Stephen was kind of 'persona non gratia' when I introduced him to my family but seeing as we were older and

I'm a bit of a rebel anyway, when it came out we were living together, whoa… out with the garlic! and not married…' she made speech marks with her fingers. 'Well that sealed my fate as an undesirable daughter! They've not had much to do with us since. Listen leave me your address or number and we'll keep in touch okay.'

Shamir smiled and nodded, 'That would be so good and we'd like you to meet Stephen.'

The two women embraced, then as they drew apart Nita says.

'Go and get something to eat and it's been so good to see you both, take care and good luck with the pregnancy!'

Nita stood and continued her route towards the bay window and the family. Standing by the two tables she smiled watching everyone. Harold and Sylvie were ploughing their way through two plates of food; chicken legs, sausages on sticks, pork pie, a selection of bread soldiers with different toppings and taking crisps from a bowl on the table. Harold looked at Nita and grinned.

'Aye Nita this is a good spread, get yur'sel some afore it's all gone!'

Richard slipped out from his seat, putting his arm around her shoulder.

'You sit there while I get you another drink and Angus,' he prodded him in the ribs, 'goes and gets you something to eat.'

She began to say something… but Richard interrupted her.

'No, no argument you sit, we want to see you eat something, okay!'

She allowed herself to be led to sit next to Emma who was feeding the twins little bits of sandwich and sausage roll and some salad pieces which they were enjoying, while sitting on Marys' and their other Grandma, Elspeth's knees. Granddad Iain and Uncle Stewart appeared to Nita to be spending their time going backwards and forwards either to the bar or dining room to replenish everyone's drinks and plates of food.

Emma glanced at her.

'I know you must be sick of this, but are you alright?'

'Mmm yes, I've met so many people who've had such lovely things to say about Stephen, it's kind of helped me through this afternoon.'

'Good, take heart from that, everyone here has their own memories of him and how he touched their lives either through work or *Finbar*.'

She stroked Emma's thigh affectionately.

'You have to take the same pleasure from this too Em, he really seems to have been some sort of Saint according to those who knew him. The number of people whose paths he crossed over the years that remember him giving them a hand or simply showing new drivers short-cuts to make the job easier. The man we knew had an even bigger heart than we ever imagined. The difference is Em, you and I had his love and affection as the bonus ball.'

They grinned at one another nodding, Nita turned as Richard put a drink in front of her and Angus brought her a plate of food. He was laughing quietly as he placed it in front of her.

'You would not believe that dining room, it's like someone released some locusts in there. Nearly everything's been eaten.'

Richard laughed, commenting, 'Truck drivers you know, they're a bit like camels only its food with them not water. It's because they don't know where the next meal's coming from, they've got hollow legs to store it in.'

Angus and Richard laughed again when Stewart added.

'Hahaha listen, you know when you see them parked up in lay-by's… they're ruminating like cows ready for the next leg of the drive.'

All three were getting silly now, attracting some attention from those standing near them as they laughed aloud.

'Hahaha next leg, that's funny,' Richard said, 'do you think they walk with a limp until they empty the other full one! Hahaha'

Nita and Emma glared at the three men feeling a little embarrassed by their behaviour, when Mary said firmly and quite loudly,

'Richard, boys enough! Behave yourselves, you're showing us all up and setting the twins a bad example!'

The men quietened down and the volume from the general conversation around them began to build up again. Mary shrugged at Nita and Emma and smiled.

'We're going to have to watch those three, the lads are a bad influence on Richard they get him into all sorts of trouble; it's like he's going through some sort of age crisis. Have you noticed whenever they get together the child comes out in them?'

Mary, Elspeth, Nita and Emma all agreed. Nita shuffled to the end of the window seat and stood up.

'Right I'm going to meet some more of these folk I've not said hello too yet, I'll be back.'

Halfway across the bar she felt a tap on her shoulder, turning she was faced by the Superintendent and Ruth.

'Lovie we're going to have to get off, just wanted to say thank you this was a lovely do. You know where we are, any time Nita call okay?'

Superintendent Allen added.

'When you're ready Nita we need to see you with the doctor to discuss bringing you back to work.' He touched her arm gently, 'No hurry, in your own time okay? And there's another matter we can deal with then but not before you're ready alright.'

She felt a shiver run through her and a sense of extreme tiredness wash over her, she reached for the back of a chair just to support herself until she'd recovered her composure again. Ruth stood by her suddenly concerned and held her an arm, Nita glanced at her.

'Thanks, are you going to tell me what happened and how…'

Her voice trailed off and she just looked from one to the other, too tired to speak, the superintendent said quietly.

'Not before you are ready detective I mean it there's no rush.'

Ruth tightened her hold on Nita's arm and said, smiling at her.

'Like I just said lovie we are all here for you, Alan will keep us up to speed so there'll be no getting away or shutting yourself off.'

Smiling back at her, she said.

'I know and I will, thank you for coming today, you too sir. Say thanks to Alan and Linda will you and everyone back at the office, I've had some lovely cards and messages.'

One more squeeze from Ruth and the two officers left her joining the others waiting to leave, she raised her arm to wave to them.

Standing alone now she suddenly experienced a huge feeling of isolation. A sense of panic took hold of her, she turned back towards the bar and dining room searching for someone. The feeling of panic continued to grow as the person she wanted she couldn't see, she was breathing heavily now. Christine and a couple of the drivers walked out of the bar coming towards her, Chris began to say something when she realised Nita was obviously distressed about something. Taking her arm she spoke to her calmly.

'Nita, Nita what's the matter love?'

'Stephen, I can't find Stephen Chris, do you know where he's gone? I can't see him anywhere!'

Leading her away from the reception area by the bar towards the seat at the bottom of the stairs, she turned to one of the guys who'd followed her.

'Stan go and find Emma quickly!'

'Where?' he asked.

'Use your bloody head man,' she said firmly, 'she was with the family in the window seats.'

'Oh right, okay.'

To the other man there she said, 'Get some water from the bar.'

Moments later Emma, Angus and Mary appeared in the hallway closely followed by Jean.

Chris stood by Emma.

'I think she's perhaps having some sort of a panic attack, she was hyper-venting when…'

Nita spoke, her voice strained with emotion.

'Emma I can't see your dad, do you know where he's gone. I've asked Chris but she doesn't know either.'

Her breathing was becoming short and laboured again. Emma knelt by her side holding her arm and gently stroking her thigh.

'It's alright Nita, do you remember we were at the church this morning for a special service for Stephen and now we're at the Duchess with all his friends and work mates for lunch.'

She stared blankly at Emma, it was as though there was no recognition in her eyes. She looked at the others around her in the hall, Angus said quietly.

'There are too many people here she needs space, can I suggest we think about getting her home now before she loses it totally.'

'I'm cold… its cold Emma, I'm tired I want to sleep.'

Jean turned going back to the bar as Emma stood up and nodded to Angus.

'You're right she can't cope anymore; okay let's get her home pronto.'

Jean re-appeared from the bar handing Mary a soft blanket which she wrapped around Nita's shoulders.

'Thank you.' Mary acknowledged Jean.

'Let me have it back sometime duck.'

Chris meanwhile and the two drivers had moved towards the door. She called quietly to Emma.

'Em, we were just coming to say good-bye and thank you, what a wonderful send off for him. Let us know how she is later will you?

Angus set off to follow them out.

'I'll bring the car round to the front,

Emma nodded, then to Christine replied.

'Thank you Chris I'm glad you all made it, yes I'll let you know how she goes on.'

'Okay, bye.'

Mary glanced at Emma.

'Can I suggest you get the girls and the three of us get her home? You stay with the twins and Angus tonight, I think they need you and you need a night free of stress.'

Emma held Mary's look, thinking for a few moments.

'That would be lovely actually, but I feel guilty leaving all of you to look after Nita.'

'Em listen to me, since the accident you've virtually lived here, you need a break. The girls know Nita, we're all family, stay with your family tonight, rest sweetheart.'

Emma nodded still looking at Mary, who smiled at her granddaughter.

'The correct answer is yes nan!'

Emma grinned broadly, replying, 'Yes nan, thank you.'

'Good, now go and get the girls and find Richard for me.'

As she turned to go back to the bar Angus came through the front doors. Mary looked towards Emma shooing her away with back of her hand.

'Go, get the girls.'

By the time the three of them returned with Richard and Nita's pashmina and bag, Mary had filled Angus in with tonight's plan. She quickly brought Richard up to speed as the girls helped Nita down the steps of the Duchess and into the car.

'I'll see you back at the hotel darling,' he called. 'Tell mum and dad what's happening, yeah?'

'I will. Look after her, call me if …'

'Absolutely not!' Louise called from the passenger seat, 'night off girl, enjoy it.'

Mary, Emma and Richard waved them off then returned to the gathering. Emma went to the bar to tell Jean what was happening. Meanwhile Mary and Richard sat back at the window tables to bring the others up to speed. Stewart listened to the plans eventually saying in his soft Scots dialect.

'Should you not be calling the Doc back, this sounds to me more like a breakdown.'

Emma, back to the table from the bar now asked.

'Breakdown, what about a breakdown?'

Elspeth began to say, 'Stewart was wondering…' when Stewart spoke over her.

'I was wondering as it's been nearly three months now and she doesn't seem to be showing any real signs of a recovery. Perhaps today's events, the service and here has just brought everything to a head and maybe caused this breakdown.' He sighed and finished saying, 'The meds she's on are helping short term but she's basically surviving on a day to day basis. There has to be something else they can do Em, to get her through this!'

Emma thought for a moment.

'Okay yes, let's see how she is tomorrow and I'll speak to the Doctor on call and see what he recommends.'

The family started to gather all their bits and pieces together, bags, books, the twin's crayons and toys, Elspeth turned to Emma asking quietly.

'How are we going to do this Emma? Should Iain and I take the twins, we've got the children's seats in our car. Do you want to come in ours and I'll go back with Stewart, Harold and Sylvie?'

Emma turns to the two children.

'Granddad Iain is taking you back to the hotel, do you want me to come too or go with Granny?'

The twins' glance at the two adults momentarily, then reply almost in unison, 'Granny!!' they shout.

Grinning Emma looks at Elspeth.

'That answer your question?'

All the grownup's chuckle at the enthusiastic reply from the two little ones. Gathering some of the bags together, Iain says.

'Right, we'll get off then and see you back at the hotel.'

Elspeth follows him with the twins, stroking Emma's shoulder as she passes her.

'Take your time sweetheart, there's no rush, okay.'

'Mmm thanks.'

Harold and Sylvie get to their feet and slowly make their way through the bar to the door.

'I'll get them into the car Emma alright.'

Stewart says as he turns to follow them out, carrying the remaining bags and bits.

'Okay, will you take them back to the hotel please my lovely man I want few minutes, I just want a word with a couple of folk still here.' He studies her for a moment, recognising a certain look in her eye and nods.

Walking to the bar she pulls a stool towards the end of the bar where Mick Holmes has stood since they'd all arrived from the church.

Jean comes to her. 'What'll it be mi' duck?'

Studying the optics and the shelf holding the array of spirits behind Jean's head, she says eventually.

'Have you a Speyside single malt other than the Glen Fiddich?'

Taking a tumbler from beneath the bar, she turns to the shelf, moves one or two bottles until she finds a particular one. Taking a measure she pours a double into a glass and over her shoulder says, 'Water, ice or both?'

'Just enough water to cut it please.'

Taking a jug from the bar she empties it before running a tap for a few moments and refills it. Placing the tumbler in front of her she puts the jug by its side then takes two more glasses putting a measure in each from one of the optics, passing one to Mick. She raises her glass then glances at Mick and Emma.

'To a true gent and friend, rest in peace.'

Mick simply nods, 'Amen to that.'

They both drink the amber liquid, Emma raises her glass in silence. The three of them sit for some time feeling the warmth of the spirit slowly working its way inside them. Finally Emma breaks the silence.

'Thank you… both, that was perfect.'

They continue to sit quietly for a while until Jean looking up at the clock at the side of the bar says.

'I need to do a couple of things before we open, okay?'

Emma smiles, 'Sorry Jean, I'm just sitting here getting a little morose.' Turning to Mick she says. 'I know how you, dad and Nita first met but not much else except he'd moor up at the old wharf whenever he was travelling up and down the river.'

'Aye, he made quite an entrance that first time. To be honest love I thought he were a right amateur with heaps of cash to throw at a boat just to look good.' He chuckled briefly, 'Just goes to shows how a posh name can make a fool of you. Did he ever talk about someone called Joe?'

Emma thought for a moment.

'Don't think so, where does he fit into all this then?'

'He were the master of one of the NCB colliers and just like me, because your dad had a double-barrelled name, thought he was up himself too. Fooled us all really, just a normal top guy and a bit of a hero to boot I suppose. Tell you what, Nita were a stunner! well still is, I got your dad to come and stay here for one night after the attack just to rest his ribs. He were in a right mess Emma, he should've stayed in hospital a day or two longer but he was hell-bent on getting *Finbar* down the river. Any-roads he gets talking to Nita and invites her here for dinner, he'd asked if I'd like a drink to say thanks, you know for helping sort stuff out. I turned up and they were both nattering away over there by the fire. Tell you what, she was wearing something like what she had on today… stunning… drop dead gorgeous.' he called to Jean, 'Weren't she Jean, Nita, drop dead gorgeous that night he stayed here.' Jean nodded as Mick carried on with his story. Emma smiled to herself she was beginning to feel much happier in herself listening to someone she hardly knew relate how they and others saw her dad and how much they thought of him. She listened as Mick related Stephens September meeting with Nita at the wharf.

'I knew it were serious then and I was right, seven years… Eee a tragedy! I can't tell you how sorry I am love, truly.'

She reached the short distance across the bar to him, held his arm giving it a squeeze.

'Thank you Mick, I haven't heard much about how they met. None of the family really got to know Nita until that first Christmas then there was the Easter we spent in York. That was when we saw the real Nita.' almost to herself she added quietly, 'Now we've got to get her through this, god knows how!'

A soft Scottish voice spoke close to her ear.

'And we will with his help.'

Emma jumped, spinning round on her seat side-swiping Angus in the process who'd taken a step back.

'You sod!' she scolded him, 'I've told you before about sneaking up on me, stop doing it!'

Turning to Mick she saw he was grinning broadly and scowled at him.

'You knew he was there, why didn't you tell me!'

Mick shrugged, 'He shushed me when he came round the corner.'

'I hate you … both of you!'

Angus went over to Mick and held his hand out, 'I'm Angus, Angus Farquhar pleased to meet you. How do you know this charming lady may I ask?'

'Mick Holmes,' he replied, 'I knew her dad quite well and Nita, I was just telling Emma how the three of us met.'

Angus nodded and glanced back to Emma.

'Are you ready or would you like another…,' he lifted the empty tumbler and sniffed the remnants in the bottom of the glass, '… whisky?'

Emma smiled coyly at him, 'That would be nice but I think I'd like to go please.'

'Okay, you can have another when we get back to the hotel.'

She slipped off the stool and moved to stand by Mick, he straightened himself up as she put her arms round his very broad shoulders and kissed his cheek. From the other end of the bar Jean called out.

'Put him down Emma, you don't know where he's been!'

Stepping back she said quietly, 'Thank you for the insight Mick, you've coloured in a lot of dad's life.'

'My pleasure love, any time.'

Moving along the bar to where Jean was serving some regulars, she waited.

'Jean, we can't thank you enough for accommodating us and all that you've done arranging this today it's been absolutely wonderful we are so grateful. Now are you sure that the cost has been covered, do we owe you more?'

Jean came around the bar and put her arms around each of their waists guiding them towards the door.

'It's all covered mi' duck, we here, all of us are so sorry for your loss it's truly tragic. The little we knew of Stephen we soon realised he really was one of the good guys, you could say he was an honorary local. I know you aren't locals either but you're all welcome here whenever you're in the area, okay?'

Giving Emma a final squeeze around her waist she released them watching as they walked through the ornate doors and down the steps of the pub.

Chapter Five

As Angus drove them back through Portbridge to the hotel he glanced at Emma periodically and saw her shoulders gradually relax as the tension she'd been showing through the day eased. He smiled as he saw her beautiful soft features return to her face again. She became aware of his glances.

'What?'

'Oh nothing my lovely lady, I've just watched all the stress of today leave you. Right now you look so much like your mum does in the pictures we have around the house… just beautiful!'

She gave a soft huff smiling affectionately at him. Arriving back at the hotel they walked into the bar to see Mary, Richard, Iain, Elspeth and Stewart sitting around a table with tea things covering it. Of the twins there wasn't sight or sound.

'Okay what have you done with my little Angels?' Emma said.

Quick as a flash Stewart replied without looking at Emma or his brother.

'Got this couple passing the hotel to take them off your hands, they thought they were lovely. Got a great price for them too…' A ripple of laughter ran around the table.

'Yeah right,' Emma said, 'well you can just go and give them their money back Stewart Farquhar, they are not for sale!'

Stewart quickly looked up at Emma, the tone of her voice getting his attention immediately. He saw her eyes firmly focused on him and shuffled under her stare, then relaxed when he saw her lift an eyebrow and saw a soft grin spread across her face. Angus ginned at his brother.

'Be careful brother, that's a side of this lady you wouldn't want to see very often, trust me.'

The laughter ran around the table again as Mary leant towards him saying quietly.

'That's her mum coming out, it was the only way she could get Stephen to be sensible when he'd got one of his feather-brained ideas in his head. We never saw it in Emma until she met you two at Uni and witnessed some of the brainless antics you both got involved in.' glancing at Angus briefly, she added, 'Right?'

Angus nodded, Emma repeated her question, 'Where are they then?'

Elspeth said, 'They fell asleep coming back here, we carried them in and they had about 40 minutes. Harold and Sylvie have taken them to the restaurant for tea and offered to baby-sit tonight so we can have a meal together before we all head off tomorrow.'

'Are they alright with that, they must be pretty tired themselves.' Emma said.

Elspeth carried on, 'We thought so but they were insistent, what do you think?'

Richard commented, 'Well, we'll all be here so if they start to play up one of us can go and help. I asked Harold if they were okay looking after them, he said this would be the last time he and Sylvie would be able to spend some time with them just on their own.'

Emma looked at Angus for a moment.

'What do you think darling, if we bath them and do stories they should sleep, it's been a busy day for them.'

'Yeah if we do the bedtime bit, they'll be okay with Harold and

Sylvie and like Richard says we're here and can help if needs be.'

Emma turned, setting off towards the dining room, 'I'll have a word okay.'

Sometime later the twins rushed into the lounge followed by the three grown-ups. Confidently they mingled among their grandparents each trying to outdo the other in telling tales on their sibling about what they'd eaten or who did what in the dining room. Angus called the twins to come and sit between Emma and himself explaining the bedtime plan to them. In the meantime Richard had ordered fresh tea which duly arrived at their table. Mary assumed the role of 'mother' pouring tea for Harold and Sylvie before topping up everyone else's cups. It wasn't long before the two children began to show signs of tiredness, each resting on a parent, Elspeth smiled saying quietly to Mary.

'I think they're finished for the day just look at the darlings.'

Angus looked across to Rory snuggled against Emma, his eyelids heavy and drooping as he struggled to fight off sleep.

'Em,' he nodded to the recumbent body nestled against her.

'Bath and bed I think.'

She nodded and they each scooped up a child saying softly to them.

'Say night to everyone.'

Ever so faintly they all heard them say.

'Night night,' as they left the lounge.

'I'll give you a call when they're in bed, okay?' Emma said over her shoulder, Harold waved briefly.

At eight-pm with Harold and Sylvie settled in Emma and Angus' room keeping an eye on the two slumbering children with an array of sandwiches and drinks to keep them company, the remainder of the family gathered in the bar until they were called to their table. The evening passed quietly as they enjoyed their dinner relaxing talking through all that had happened; about how it had affected each of them but more importantly how they could help and support Nita in the coming weeks. Obviously, for all of them it would have to be long distance support from their own homes and whilst there were the girls, Louise and Moira on hand, it wouldn't be right for them to take on the overall responsibility of being Nita's shadows until she was capable of facing the future on her own. If asked they all thought the girls would no doubt make themselves available to take the lead in the short term, but everybody agreed that whilst they could be the 'go to people' in first instant, it would have to be stressed that if that happened then they must call Emma, Mary or Richard and they would come up straight away. Emma and Angus said they would speak to the girls tomorrow before they left and share the family's thoughts with them, emphasising that they were not expected to take on Nita's short-term care and support alone. The question now arose as to how much close support they thought the police would give Nita over the coming weeks; generally everyone felt there wouldn't be any hesitation if they, the family, felt that a situation was developing that indicated Nita's state of mind was becoming a concern and they needed more professional help for her. Emma pointed out that the detective section in Portbridge had always seemed to her to be a really tight group who were detectives first, and family second and felt they could be relied on to close ranks around Nita to support her.

Later the subject of *Finbar* came up and what was to become of her. Since Emma and Angus had first introduced each other to their prospective in-laws, the summer cruises had returned to 3 or 4 weeks around the English coast, more specifically the inner and Outer Hebrides. For convenience when she wasn't in use she was moored at one or the other end of the Crinan canal. Stephen and Nita had just brought her back to the Grahams yard for the winter before he'd left for this last trip. Everyone felt that for the moment the boat wasn't a priority but Emma said she'd speak to Robert Graham and ask his advice.

It was approaching 11pm when Mary and Richard finally admitted that they were past it and were off to bed, closely followed by Elspeth and Iain. Stewart suggested a final nightcap for the three of them, but Emma declined feeling she ought to go and relieve Harold and Sylvie and left the boys to adjourn to the bar. On returning to their room she was 'de-briefed' as to how the evening had gone and how good the twins had been. They were just leaving the room when Angus came down the corridor with Stewart. Alone in their room they shared a whisky Angus had brought with him and relaxed for a while before getting ready for bed. In the corner of the room the twins were sleeping top-to-tail on the occasional bed used in the family room. Emma watched them for a few moments smiling to herself. Climbing in beside Angus she snuggled up to him, he kissed her pulling her closer.

'You did so well today darling, they'd both be so proud of you. I love you Em.'

From the slumbering body beside him he heard a soft sigh and a faint reply.

'Love you too.'

Chapter Six

The morning at the hotel revealed scenes bordering a military exercise. Following a family breakfast, suitcases and bags were packed into cars; Harold and Sylvie's cases were brought to the foyer ready for the taxi to take them to the station for their train back to York. Stewart offered to run them there as he would be passing close by on his run home to East Yorkshire. Harold thanked him then added.

'We've got our passes and the home have a mini bus that'll pick us up from the station so we'll travel door to door. We both like a train journey son, it reminds us of our youth when there were trains to everywhere; not like these days you know.'

There were hugs and kisses all round, especially for the twins as everyone said their farewells when the taxi arrived. The twins excitedly ran to Emma and Angus to show them a shiny pound coin Harold had given each of them.

'Did you say thank you?' Angus said to them as Emma looked at Harold pointing her finger at him.

'That wasn't necessary grandpa,' she said, '… but thank you.'

Theirs was a special embrace as they said goodbye.

'You take care of yourself our Emma do you hear! It's going to take time lass you know that but you're strong and you've got a good man there, lean on him all right.' giving her another extra hug he said, 'Love you our Em.'

Returning his hug she replied, 'Love you too grandpa.'

Harold turned to Angus shaking his hand as Emma hugged Sylvie, who said.

'Don't you worry love, I'll see he's all right. You concentrate on you and those two gorgeous babies of yours.'

'Thank you Sylvie I will. We'll come up to see you both in a while when all the dust has settled.'

Sylvie patted her hand as she got into the taxi and they all watched it drive off. An hour later Mary and Richard left with Iain and Elspeth close behind them. Later Emma and Angus and the twins drove through Portbridge to the house where Louise met them.

'Morning.' Louise said cheerfully as they all trooped into the hallway.

'Yes morning,' Emma replied embracing her, 'How was last night, alright?'

'Morning.' Angus added as he was the last through the door.

Louise crouched down to the twins standing just behind Emma's legs shyly.

'Hello you two, are you alright this morning?'

They nodded in unison then timidly edged past Louise into the lounge. Standing again she answered Emma.

'Yeah last night was good. Tea coffee, name it.' She clicked the switch on the kettle and continued. 'She slept well, woke maybe twice but no real dramas. She was up with me and Moira had some breakfast then went back to bed when Moira left for work. I have to say she actually looked rested this morning. She's only had one set of tablets that was when we got home last night. I'll take a drink up for her now when I make yours. How were you last night?'

'Fine thanks, just being with himself and the family made a huge difference, thank you.'

The two women giggled briefly. From the other side of the breakfast bar where Angus was standing keeping an eye on the twins, he said softly.

'What am I being accused of now, hmm?'

'Nothing my lovely man, except for just being a wonderful person.'

'Oh okay, I can live with that.'

The women giggled again, Louise placed a teapot and cafetiere on the bar.

'Help yourselves, there's milk in the fridge and sugar here.' she said pushing a small bowl towards them. 'I'll take this up to Nita and let her know you're here.'

Pouring a coffee into a mug she disappeared upstairs.

Emma poured a tea for herself and a coffee for Angus'

'Drink sweetheart,' she said pushing a mug across the surface of the bar.

'Thank you. I'll put the tele on for the twins is that alright?'

'Fine, it'll entertain them for a bit until we've talked to Louise.'

From the bottom of the stairs Louise asked.

'Talk to me about what?' then to the twins she said, 'Do you want to go and see Nani, she's all cosy and warm in bed.'

The two children dashed from the lounge and scrambled up the stairs shouting as they went.

'Nani, Nani.'

From the kitchen the three of them could just hear lots of animated chatter and giggles.

'That'll get her going.' Louise commented, 'Talk to me about what?'

Over the next half hour Emma and Angus talked through what the family had discussed the previous evening, stressing that neither Louise nor Moira were Nita's carers and until she was in a better place it was paramount they call and someone would be back here within the day. The important thing was, whilst the three of them had all lived together they each had their own lives and careers and they must come first. Before the conversation could move on they were aware that Nita was coming down to join them, preceded by the thunder of little feet on the stairs. Turning to come into the kitchen at the foot of the stairs she said.

'Hello you two, are you ready to go back down south then?'

Emma went to embrace her thinking she looked better than over the past few days, although her face still showed the strain. She looked pale and gaunt even though she'd brushed her hair and put some make-up on, she could see she'd lost a lot of weight.

'No,' she replied, 'remember, we said we'd stay until the weekend and help sort stuff out if you felt up to it.'

Nita nodded vacantly, but honestly couldn't remember that conversation. Elizabeth came to her side tugging at her jumper.

'Nani come and sit with Rory and me.'

Taking her hand she pulled Nita away into the lounge, Emma and Louise smiled briefly.

'Darling will you go to the car,' Emma said, 'and bring the bags we need and then I think we ought to do something about lunch. Louise what are your plans for the rest of the day, were you staying on here or going back to the house?'

'Depending on whether or not you were going to be staying as you'd planned earlier in the week,' Louise said, 'we were staying tonight. Moira's coming here anyway then I suppose we could go back to the house.'

'If that's okay with you both then I would like to stay 'til the weekend, just to see how she settles now we've had the service.'

Louise nodded, 'Okay, sounds like a plan. Do we need another get together before you go, to see how she's coping?'

Thinking for a moment Emma said, 'Not really, but we'll make a point of seeing you both before we go anyway. Now lunch, who fancies what?'

She waited for a response from someone; from the front door, which Angus had just crashed through laden with bags and toys, he said.

'Fish and chips from that shop at the end of what's-it street!'

Emma and Louise laughed, Emma saying.

'What's-it Street… where exactly is that then?'

Angus persisted, 'You know, on the way to the off-shop.'

From the lounge they heard Nita say.

'Duckworth Street, at the junction with Gainsborough Road.'

'That's it!' Angus says, 'fish and chips from Duckworth Street.' With his next breath he said, 'Rory, Lizzie dripping, do you want your toys?'

The children came to him as he stooped, allowing them to take some soft toys and books from the top of the bags.

'If you go and ask Nani nicely she might read you a story.'

Emma said scowling at him for a moment.

'I do wish he wouldn't call her that.'

Smiling Louise said.

'Oh Emma it's so sweet the way he says it, in those soft tones it sounds so loving and affectionate.'

Emma glanced at Louise and grimaced gritting her teeth as if to imply… thanks for your support! they both laugh.

The fish and chips duly arrived; Emma and Louise were relieved to see Nita eat her portion, it being the first substantial meal they'd seen her eat for almost a week. A little later she said she was feeling tired with all the hubbub from Elizabeth and Rory and was going for a rest. With a little gentle encouragement, Emma and Angus got the twins to take a nap at the same time in 'mummy's old bedroom'. Alone again the three of them continued to discuss the best way to support Nita over the coming weeks until she felt she was ready to return to work. Sorting through Stephens's things came up next, they all agreed she ought to have at least one of them with her when the time came to face that task. It needed someone to support her should something come up which might bring on a surge of emotion whether it be some documents, clothes or special mementoes. Emma and Angus reiterated again that while she and Moira were good friends of the family they weren't expected to take on that roll alone and one of family would come and stay with her. The latter part of the afternoon was spent sitting around in the cosy lounge playing games with the twins, watching children's programmes on television or reading books? Just after five Moira arrived back and after a brief chat she and Louise left with Emma arranging to see them before they travelled back to Bristol. After baths for the twins and Nani reading stories for them, they settled down and slept. Nita, Emma and Angus sat quietly in the lounge.

Wandering off into the kitchen a little later, Angus found the bottle of malt whiskey, pouring three good measures for them.

'I'm not sure I should be drinking this,' Nita said as she took the tumbler from him, 'bearing in mind the meds I'm supposed to be taking.'

'Wheest woman, it's medicinal!' he said.

She looked across to Emma who was smiling and catching her eye saw her briefly raise an eyebrow and shrug her shoulders.

'I don't think one will do you any harm.'

She took a sip and sighed.

'Oh that's lovely, I could get used to this you know.'

They all giggled briefly, then Emma said.

'How do you feel in yourself just now?'

She sat for a few moments studying the amber liquid in her glass then glanced across to Emma.

'I don't really know Em, it's been a nice day with you all here, the house felt happy, lived in… do you understand. It's like, since the accident, it's had this empty…' She hesitated for a moment searching for a way to describe what she was trying to say. 'No, it's more than that, its felt cold, I've had this feeling of being a stranger like I shouldn't be here, can you understand that?'

Emma looked at Angus briefly and then back at Nita as she continued.

'Today's been a good day really I've felt more me, more normal, I actually felt like I could move on a little, face the world again.'

'That's good to hear, I have to say I thought you've been more with us today and yes the house has felt more like it's old self.'

The three of them sat in silence for a while sipping their drinks listening to the sounds around the house. Emma sighed taking a breath and began to say to Nita,

'You've just said you feel in a better place today.' Nita nodded, 'we've planned to stay over the weekend. I want you to be honest, how do you think you'll manage when we've gone, do you feel you'll be strong enough to cope with each day?'

Nita shrugged, 'I honestly can't say, I don't think I've had the dream for the last two nights so right now I feel l could manage, the test will be when you all drive off into the sunset….'

She stopped talking and sobbed aloud, her face contorted and both she and Angus saw the strain instantly return. They watched her concerned, wondering what had just happened. Emma went across the room and sat beside her taking her hand in hers.

'What just happened Nita?' she waited for an answer, all the time watching Nita's face for any signs. She asked again. 'Nita talk to me, what's just happened?'

Nita shivered visibly, then looking at Emma said softly, her voice cracking with emotion.

'Right… after your dad and I had spent that first weekend on *Finbar*, we both kind of knew there was something special between us and I asked him if this was going to be it. Was he going to drive off into… the sunset… never to be seen again?'

Putting her arms around her Emma drew her into an embrace and felt her shake as she broke into tears. She held her close for some time until she became calm.

'Nita you're so much a part of this family, you gave me back my dad remember and for that I can't thank you enough. So we are not going to disappear into the sunset ever we'll be back to mess with your head and your life whenever we can, believe it… yes!'

Giving Emma a squeeze she lifted her head from her chest and through watery eyes smiled at her stroking her cheek gently.

'You know I couldn't have got through these last weeks without you and Angus of course, you are an amazing woman, so strong Em like your dad, thank you.'

They hugged once more then sat quietly together on the settee, Angus replenished his drink and Emma's but they decided that one was enough for Nita. It wasn't long before she said goodnight to the two of them and went off to bed. Within the hour Angus and Emma followed her, moving the twins from their bed to their make-shift beds, two bottom draws from the old chest in their room. Giggling softly Emma whispered to Angus.

'I guess we won't be able to do this again, it makes you realise how they've grown since we were last here.'

In the other bedroom Nita lay cuddling her bear listening to the gentle sounds from the spare bedroom. She smiled reflecting on part of the conversation the three of them had had earlier. She squeezed her bear tightly thinking that, yes tonight the house did feel warm and welcoming for the first time in almost four months. Very shortly with everyone sleeping peacefully, the house fell silent and Nita finally slept.

Angus quietly slipped out of bed and crept down the stairs intending to begin making breakfast and drinks for everyone. Going into the kitchen, he was surprised to see Nita in her dressing gown slumped across the breakfast bar fast asleep. Gently he reached out to touch the mug by her side, it was stone cold, he said softly not wanting to shock or surprise her.

'Nita,' he waited a moment then repeated himself, 'Nita… how long have you been down here?'

She stirred, groaning softly and pushed herself a little more upright groaning again, Angus repeated himself.

'How long have you been down here, are you not cold woman?'

She sat up properly, stretching and gently gyrating her upper body to ease her stiffness, Angus asked again.

'How long have you been down here?'

Turning, she looked at the wall clock and then at Angus.

'Ohh just before five I think, I woke up in a sweat and wanted a drink so l came down and made some tea.'

'Had you slept until then?'

'Mmm yeah, I think I've had a reasonable night.'

Filling the kettle he clicked it on and set about sorting out the teapot and some mugs. Upstairs came the sound of children giggling and Emma squealing playfully. Nita glanced at him smiling but he saw sadness in her eyes.

'Stephen was so proud of Em you know and you too and he simply adored the twins, He couldn't believe it when they were born he was so made up for you both. He got quite emotional you know when he saw them for the first time, he said to me that he wished Suzanne could have seen how well Emma had grown up and how good you two were together, the twins were the topping on the cake.'

He crossed to the breakfast bar gently caressing her shoulder, looking into his eyes she covered his hand on her shoulder with hers, he saw her eyes were full of tears. Passing her a tissue from the box on the worktop he put a fresh mug of tea beside her.

'I know we're leaving today but as Em said yesterday we're only a phone call away. Don't be a hero and suffer on your own, you call us okay! We love you to bits, you know you are so much a part of the twins' lives they talk about you and grampy all the time.'

Any further conversation was pointless as the patter of tiny feet on the stairs grew into a thunder as Rory and Elizabeth ran into the kitchen and together said to Angus excitedly.

'Daddy daddy, mummy say's we have to say she's waiting for her morning cup of tea!'

Both Angus and Nita looked at one another and laughed. He set the two children on a stool each and pouring tea into a mug set off upstairs saying to the twins.

'Decide what you would like for breakfast and ask Nani to help you.'

By lunchtime all their bags, toys and bits were packed into the people carrier ready to drive back to Bristol. The twins were watching some children's television and the three adults were sitting around the breakfast bar sipping tea.

'As much as I love you all,' Nita said reaching for Emma's hand smiling at her.

'I don't want you to delay leaving just because it means I'm on my own. I have to start getting used to being here on my own.'

'Are you sure you're up to this just now?' Emma asked.

She nodded, squeezing her hand.

'I'm sure…' Both Emma and Angus studied her, 'I'm sure… okay.' she replied as confidently as possible.

'Look whilst you two were upstairs this morning and the twins were happy eating their breakfast I phoned Louise, she and Moira are coming around tonight and I'm going to cook for us all, all right…! I'm going to be okay… okay!'

'Right,' Angus said decisively, 'the decisions been made come on let's get this show on the road.'

Emma glanced at him sternly, a look Nita saw.

'He's right Em you need to go or we'll still be sitting here at teatime.'

Slipping off her stool she walked round to Emma and put her arms around her, the two women gently hugged one another for quite some time; when the separated they both had tears in their eyes.

'Em we have to start somewhere or we'll never move on. You've been amazing I don't know where you've got the strength from to carry on over the past weeks and months but without you, god knows how

I'd have got here.'

Emma nodded unable to speak, dabbing her eyes with a tissue. Still holding each other Nita said softly.

'We'll never forget him Em, just as you and dad never forgot your mum. Think Emma, we all spoke about her just as though she'd left the room, we have to remember dad like that now.'

Nodding she replied, 'I know, but us leaving is like an end and that's hard Nita.'

'Yes, Em it is but it's also a beginning too.' gently stroking her cheek, 'Listen neither of us can move on until we face tomorrow as a new day. Come on lovely let's get you on your way and then we can begin.'

They walked to the front door where Nita reached out taking her arm firmly.

'Emma, I couldn't have survived this without you being here with me, for that I will forever thank you.'

She drew her into another tight embrace. Two pairs of arms suddenly wrapped themselves round the girl's legs, they looked down at two bright faces grinning at them both. Nita reached down and first picked up Rory and kissed him then Elisabeth.

'Listen to me you two rascals, I want you to promise me that you are going to be very good for mummy and daddy. It's a long way home and they have to concentrate, alright?'

Elisabeth nodded saying, 'We will Nani promise.' hugging Nita's legs again.

She kissed Angus and embraced him.

'Like I said this morning,' he said, 'don't be silly and try to be a hero, if things get messy you call us!'

She nodded letting her arm slide from his shoulder as he stepped onto the street taking the twins to the car. She turned to Emma.

'We love you okay!' Emma said.

'I know, listen be careful call me when you get home okay.'

'I will, have a good night with the girls give them our love.'

Standing in the doorway she watched them settling in the car, they all waved as they drove past the house. She watched them down to the end of the street before closing the door. Walking back into the kitchen she sat on one of the bar stools listening to the growing silence in the house. Time passed the silence broken only by the steady tick-tok of the wall clock; she shook herself saying quietly. 'Come on Nita this is no good, you need to do something.' Reaching across the work surface she switched the radio on and for next few hours busied herself changing both sets of bed covers, putting the two draws the twins had slept in back in the chest. Finally she decided to make something fresh for herself and the girls tonight rather than eat take away.

By the time Moira arrived Nita had made one of the curries they loved when they all lived together. She'd showered, changed and felt relaxed looking forward to the evening. Louise eventually arrived quite a bit later and they all sat around the breakfast bar eating, chatting and sharing some wine. Later Emma called to say they'd finally got home safely. She asked how she had managed through the day and was delighted that she'd had a good day and was having an evening with her old housemates. After the phone call the three of them moved to the lounge and talked the night away until mid-night.

Over a light breakfast in the morning Louise and Moira were relieved that Nita had had a good night's sleep and seemed happy making plans for the rest of the day. As the girls left for work it was decided that Moira would pick Nita up after work and they'd all go back to their house for the evening.

Involved by Accident III: Into the Sunset

Chapter Seven

Nita felt quite apprehensive as she ascended the three flights of stairs to the office the detectives occupied in the centre of Portbridge. It was the first time she'd been back here since Stephens's accident almost seven months ago. Some time had passed since his memorial service during which she'd attended a series of meetings with the police doctor and a councillor specialising in trauma and grief counselling. Finally, the team felt that she was in a position to make a fazed return to duty. Pausing at the ornate office door, a relic from the days when the whole office block belonged to one of the smaller banks ultimately swallowed up by one of the 'big four'. She shivered slightly feeling a tingle run down her spine then, taking a deep breath she fixed her smile and opened the door. Standing inside the office she looked around to see if anything had changed. No-one really took any notice of her for quite some time, eventually Linda saw her and came across the office.

'Hello, fancy you turning up like this.'

She went to put her arms around her, Nita held her hand up to stop her but smiled.

'Don't please, I'm not quite ready yet but thank you.'

Linda returned the smile then taking her by the elbow they walked to her desk.

'Do you want a tea sweetie?'

Nita nodded, 'Oh please, my mouth is so dry, I think it's a touch of nerves to be honest.'

Looking round the office she said.

'Is Alan about?'

Linda chuckled, 'We're not worthy enough these days.'

Nita stared quizzically at her colleague, 'What?'

'Didn't you know, he's made sergeant? Stepped up two weeks ago. I thought his sister would have told you.'

Nita shook her head.

'Nope not a word but hey-ho I've had other things on my mind. Okay, is the boss in I'm supposed to see her about a fazed return to duties.'

Linda smiled broadly.

'Oh that's brilliant, it'll be like the old days again.'

'Hey hang on, this could take some time you know but I am looking forward to coming back.'

She paused for a moment then added.

'I have to move on Linda, I'm not doing myself any favours sitting around at home dwelling on everything. If I can get through this next twelve weeks and be put on real cases the distraction will help. Hopefully, I'll get some sense of perspective in my life again.'

Across the office the inspector's door opened and Ruth came out carrying her mug; walking to the breakout-area, she stopped when she saw Nita.

'Detective Patel, nice to see you again,' she gestured towards her door with her free hand, 'make yourself comfortable, I'll be with you in a minute, tea is it?'

Nita held her stare for a few moments, saw her smile softly then nodded and made her way to the Inspectors office. She smiled as she sat down, apart from the fact that everything was in neat piles on her desk and shelves, it was just the same as it had been when Superintendent Allen was the Inspector here. The same desk, same high-backed worn chair and the same old drab décor and lighting. Ruth came into the room and placed two mugs on the ring marked desktop. Closing the door she turned and pulled a file from one of the desk draws before going back to her chair. Opening it and studying the top sheet for a moment she looked directly at Nita.

'How are you coping lovie?'

'Better thanks, it's day by day you know, but yeah, better.'

Ruth looked back to the file momentarily, turned the top page and studied the document beneath for a while.

'This says you can come back to work on a fazed return to be reviewed in twelve weeks.' She glanced at Nita briefly then continued, 'It doesn't say how you are, it doesn't say how you might react to situations that might remind you of the events of the past seven months.'

She read a little more from the document, chuckled quietly before looking at Nita once more.

'It does say that any decisions to be made about your continued duties are down to your line manager. It says that a report is expected by that line manager at the review. My question to you then as your line manager is, do you feel you're ready to come back?'

Ruth stared at her now waiting for her response.

'Hhmm, put like that it sounds cold, very clinical and business like but yes I'm ready. Both of us, Emma and I realised that we had to look to the future and begin to get on with our lives. Honestly Ruth, I've been ready for the last couple of weeks but you know how slowly these wheels turn sometimes.'

'Oh yes… however in your case they had to be sure you were ready.'

Ruth sat back in her chair.

'Right, Monday 0800 then, I'll get some files for you to file and…'

She stopped and looked at Nita's stunned expression then laughed.

'Only joking lovie, Alan has a couple of things on-going so you can team up with him to begin with, will that do for starters?'

Nita grinned at her.

'Phew, you had me going then, that would be great thank you. Linda was saying he's just been made up to sergeant.'

'Yep and about time too he's been ready for ages, he'll make a good one.'

She got up to leave the office, got to the door when Ruth said.

'Listen to me! As your boss I'll be watching, do you understand! As your friend anything Nita, anything, you need you ask okay! Me, Alan, Linda, any of us; don't forget we all knew Stephen. It's going to be hard at times lovie but talk to us, you hear!'

She stood for a while looking at Ruth, then nodded.

'I will, I know it will be rough but I think I'm ready… thank you.'

'Right… sod off now, I've got a shed load of sheep sh... to sort.'

Nita grinned, 'Yes boss.'

She'd only gone a few steps when Ruth called after her.

'HEY… Shut the bloody door woman, were you born in a field!'

Nita turned back and closed the door smiling. It felt good to be back somewhere that felt familiar, with people she liked working with, doing something she loved. In the end hopefully, making the streets a better place for ordinary people. She sat with Linda for some time and they talked while Linda got on up-dating case information on her computer. Alan Syms returned to the office later in the afternoon, grinning broadly when he saw Nita sitting beside Linda.

'Well hello, aren't you a welcome sight, when do you start?'

'Monday, with you sarge!'

'A bit like the old days then, do me a favour get me a coffee will you whilst I give this lot to Linda.'

He showed a sheaf of papers to her as she moved across the office.

'Hey less of the old days,' she said over her shoulder, 'it's only seven months, but I am really looking forward to coming back.'

She made a coffee for Alan and teas for her and Linda then went to sit by Alan where he briefed her on the two cases she would be helping him with the following week. That evening, as planned, she went to Louise and Moira's for dinner where they quizzed her about the day's out-come. In the end she stayed with them for the night.

Chapter Eight

Bouncing into the office at 8am Nita half hung, half flung her coat at the stand at the entrance.

'Morning, how's everyone, how was the weekend then?'

From around the room came a selection responses, moans and groans from others already at work. Dropping her bag beside her desk she went to the breakout area making herself a drink when someone called across to her.

'Make mine a coffee, a strong one.' This was immediately followed by a second person saying, 'Make that two,' then in a louder voice added, 'Has anyone got anything for a headache… please, I'm dying here!'

Turning to see who was ordering coffee's she saw Alan and following him, Linda wearing dark glasses.

'Haven't we forgotten that little word… hmm?' Nita responded to their requests.

'Please.' Alan replied sheepishly.

Someone across the office said, 'Take more water with it in future!'

Which brought an immediate retort from Linda.

'Shut up!… It seemed like a good idea last night, I'm definitely not doing it again though.'

Nita carried the three mugs to her desk where Linda was slumped on her chair her head resting on her arms on the desktop.

'Here you are get this down you, have you had anything to eat?'

'Ohh, couldn't face anything that early.'

Reaching for the mug of coffee she took a mouthful.

'Oh god that's lovely, thank you.'

A voice called from somewhere in the office.

'Heads up… in-coming!'

This was immediately followed by a small box of tablets flying towards them which Alan Syms plucked out of the air handing it to Linda.

'Thank you whoever it was.' she called to the room.

The office door burst open as someone half crashed through it making everyone look up to see the Inspector, Ruth, stumble into the room muttering.

'I bloody hate Monday's, bloody traffic… half of them haven't got a sodding clue about lane discipline… shit for brains, all of them!'

Making her way to her own office she paused in the doorway calling to the room in general.

'Forty minutes then briefings, mine's a black coffee and a chocolate biscuit, alright!'

Pause, then just before the door closed.

'NOW!'

Reply's rippled around the room, 'Yes boss.'

By the time the traditional Monday briefing was completed everyone seemed to have got their heads clear and the tasks of the day were being addressed. As each section dispersed to pursue their enquiries the

Inspector gathered up her notes, turned to Alan Syms and said quietly.

'Alan, my office and bring Nita with you.'

A few minutes later the two of them were in front of her desk waiting to find out what she wanted from them.

'Okay Nita, you're halfway through this return to work malarkey 6 weeks now, how are you feeling, how do you think you're doing?'

A little surprised at the inspector's directness she glanced quickly at Alan. Had he said something she wondered for a moment. Taking a breath to steady the sudden surge of nerves, she replied.

'I'm doing okay l think, Alan and l have been working well together. I think we've slotted back into the groove we had before Stephen's accident. We've closed one case and passed it onto the CPS, the second one should be on your desk soon barring spanners in the works. Unless Alan has any issues about my work then I think I'm ready to return to full time duty.'

Ruth looked at Alan.

'What do you feel sergeant, is she up to a full return yet?'

'Definitely boss, this past two weeks or so she's blown off all the cobwebs, she's well up to speed again just as sharp as she ever was. She's got her nose going again sensing those little hints, nuance's you know, that feeling that something's off. As an example the case that went to CPS last week, Nita picked up on the two teenage girls' story that on the face of it looked straight forward but she saw a look between them and the older one's boyfriend. We split them up, Nita went first for the boyfriend and then the youngest girl and got a slightly bent story from the lad as to what actually happened in the alleyway at the club. When I tackled the older girl she got goby and agitated and her story fell on its face. Put together it seems she tricked the girl they attacked into leaving the club with the younger girl. After that they couldn't keep their stories together; she's ready boss, honestly.'

They both looked at Ruth waiting for a comment. She shuffled in her seat, leant forward a little and put her hands on the desktop.

'Right that answers one issue,'

Looking directly at Nita, she asked.

'Away from here lovie how are you managing. Are sleeping, eating, in short leading a fairly normal life at home?'

Nita studied her, giving herself time to form her reply aware she was going to have be careful how she answered her.

'Normal huh, I'm still trying to find normal to be honest. Yes I'm eating and surprisingly sleeping too, that's because I'm here through the day then going home tired. Being here distracts me from dwelling on what's happened. Louise and Moira have been absolute bricks, Alan knows that. I'm sure Lo has been updating him as to how I am away from here, Emma and I talk all the time, she's virtually experiencing everything I am but she's got Angus Mary and Richard as sound boards and Angus's parents too. I've got Lo and Moira and you lot here. Okay, Mary and Richard call regularly but yes boss, I'm still having the odd meltdown from time to time, that's usually triggered by something that reminds me of something we'd seen or done together, but come on Ruth it's only nine months, even the counsellors said that could happen for a year or more.'

'Are you still having the scheduled sessions with the counselling team?'

'I am Boss… what's this all about am I failing here or what? Be honest Ruth… boss, be honest?'

'Right, well I'm stuck between a rock and a hard place right now. I've watched you, heard you reasoning with Alan and broadly I agree you are ready to return to full duties. The Super has been bending my ear over the past week, he's kept his ear to the ground as well and knows how you've settled back after just six, seven weeks. Here's the rocky bit Nita, he wants you up at division working with a specialist unit that's been created to work with HMC and E and Immigration, just as you did with that Georgian, Lithuanian girl what's-her-name on the trafficking ho-hah, remember?'

Nita nodded, secretly chuffed that the work she'd done on that case had been recognised, but especially that she was being considered as part of a new team to pursue what she'd learned and bring it to this new unit; she suddenly realised that Ruth was speaking again.

'… concern lovie is, do I tell him no I need you here, that will afford you some protection from what no doubt will be quite emotional stuff at times, particularly as you're still quite vulnerable. I need to know how you feel?'

'I'm not sure,' Nita replied. 'The fact that he wants me in this unit in the first place is exciting, the prospect of helping more of these girls who've been conned, bullied, call it what you will… exploited by these gangs and ultimately putting them out of business and behind bars would be so bloody satisfying.'

Alan said thoughtfully.

'Boss can I suggest Nita has a word with the Super herself, we've all worked together he knows how thorough she is. She can go and see perhaps if it's right for her just now then make her own mind up.'

Ruth glanced at Alan and nodded.

'That's it, brilliant idea,' looking at Nita, 'Do you want me to suggest a meeting then?'

Giving a little shrug she replied.

'Well yeah I suppose nothing ventured you know.'

Both the Inspector and Alan grinned her.

'Positive thinking then!' Ruth said, 'I'll let you know in the next day or two.'

Later in the evening, at home, Nita had been speaking to Emma just as she'd done pretty well every day since everyone had gone home following Stephen's memorial service. She spoke about the days' development asking Emma what she thought, then about Emma's day. By sharing these occasions, they kept each other going; moving on dealing with how his death had affected them. She'd just walked back from the kitchen with a glass of wine and sat down again when the phone rang.

She picked it up, 'Hello'

A voice which sounded familiar but she couldn't put a name or face to just now, said.

'Nita?'

'Yes, who's this?'

'Hello pet, it's Robert, Robert Graham.'

'Robert,' she responded, 'How lovely to hear from you, how are you, how's Maggie both well l hope?'

'Whey aye pet, we're both grand you nah..'

She smiled, his Geordie accent was warm and comforting, she heard him take a breath.

'Nita pet I know we've not spoken aboot it but l want to say how sorry both of us are aboot the accident. He were a grand fella solid ya nah, reliable. We came to the service but there were so many folk there we just came home after. My Maggie was too upset to come to the pub she just felt so sorry for you and young Emma. We thought she was so brave doing the eulogy, her Da would have been proud of her, you both did so well pet.'

Feeling a sudden rush of emotion hearing Robert talking like this, she struggled to keep her voice controlled and level.

'Thank you Robert that's so kind of you to say. I think Emma did really well too, she has so much of her mum and Stephen in her. All that's happened has made her so strong.'

'True pet true, now lass ah need to talk to you aboot *Finbar*, Emma did call us just after the service but we've heard nothing more since. Now, she's out of the watter but what are we going to do with her? Ah was going to speak to Emma but Maggie thought ah'd best talk to you forst, do you want to give some thought to it and call me back in a day or two?'

Nita choked momentarily. *Finbar,* what were the family going to do with her. It had never entered her head since the day she'd heard of Stephens accident, she suddenly felt lightheaded and sick.

'Hello, are you still there Hinney… hello Nita, are you alrite pet?'

She heard Robert speaking but couldn't reply. Breathing deeply she fought back the nausea, then answered.

'Yes… yes, sorry Robert you just of threw me for a moment.'

'Ehh I'm sorry pet are you alrite?' he asked again.

Breathing easily again, she replied.

'Honestly Robert I'm okay now, it was just a bit of a shock hearing her name. To be honest it hasn't crossed my mind what to do with her, yes I'll speak to Angus first and see how he suggests we approach it with Emma. It won't be easy, after all Stephen bought her after Suzanne's death for them all to enjoy their time together as a family.'

'Aye, he always worried that everyone else was alrite forst, seldom gave a thought aboot himself just bottled it all up inside yah nah. Ehh, I'm sorry if l upset you pet, that's the last thing l meant to do.'

'Its fine Robert I'm okay now honestly. I'll get back to you as soon as I've spoken to everyone else.'

'That'll be grand pet now you look after yerself.'

'I will l promise, give Maggie my love, I'm going to come up to see you both soon.

'You're always welcome you know that, bye for now.'

'Bye Robert… and thank you.'

The line clicked and Nita replaced the handset on its rest then sat for some time thinking about how to broach the subject of *Finbar* to Emma. She smiled thinking back over the past seven years since that first summer she'd spent with the family, recalling some of the other little voyages they'd all undertaken. Even moving *Finbar* from the Grahams yard was fun, stopping off at the wharf for the night; long gone now. Mugs of tea in Mick Holmes's office and going to the Duchess for a meal. Replenishing her glass she sat down and dialled Emma's number, it rang a few times before Angus answered it.

'Hi, me again.'

'Problem?' he said

'Mmm, no not really, but maybe a bit l think.'

'Nita, are you alright, what can we do?'

She heard the concern in the tone of his voice.

'No, I mean yes I'm alright but Robert Graham has just called me, he says Emma spoke to him just after the memorial service but hasn't heard anything since. He wants to know if we have any plans for *Finbar*.'

She heard Emma in the background asking who it was calling.

'Tell you in a minute sweetheart.'

Angus said and in reply to Nita added.

'Oh yes the boat, crikey we've not given it a thought,' then asked, 'what do you think?'

'Angus, it's not really for me to decide. Stephen bought her after Suzanne died for the family to spend time together, you need to talk to Em about it and see what she thinks. I've said to Robert we'd get back to him.'

'Yes, good, leave it with me and you're sure you're okay?'

'Angus I'm fine thank you for worrying so much, it's extremely sweet of you. Right I'm turning in now, it's been a full-on day. Give my love to Rory and Elisabeth in the morning will you. Night night.'

'I certainly will, hope you sleep well, God bless.'

Hanging up, she went round the house switching everything off, checking the doors and went to bed.

Chapter Nine

The following week she was to have her review with Ruth but first she was going to Divisional HQ to see what she'd be doing if she were to join this new section DS Allen wanted her for. Driving into the car park at Division she signed in at the security desk in the lavish entrance hall that had formally been someone's grand home; she was directed to an office on the first floor. Opening the heavy ornate door she looked down a long open plan room off a long thickly carpeted corridor which she thought had possibly been the ballroom in the original house. She saw twenty or more people sitting at desks randomly spread around the room. There were two separate areas with matching easy chairs and settee's set around low tables she guessed were for informal meetings. The room was well lit by natural daylight through large ornate Georgian or Victorian windows that still had their wooden shutters set into the sides. A coffee filter machine, kettle and crockery sat on a table nestled against the wall between two of the windows. At the very end of the room was a conference table, one end of it covered with files and papers. She spun round startled when someone behind her said.

'Hello, can l 'elp you, are you looking for someone in particular?'

A woman was studying her, Nita guessed she could be around fiftyish, she looked very pale her, round face framed by her short neatly styled dark hair. She was wearing a tailored self-design light navy suit that cleverly hid the fact she was fairly plump. The open jacket revealed a soft cream coloured satin or silk blouse.

'Who is it you looking for?' they asked again.

Having recovered her composure, she replied.

'I'm meeting Detective Superintendent Allen and an Inspector Miriam Dubois and was sent to this office.'

The lady nodded. 'Right, better follow me then.'

Nita stepped back to allow the woman to pass then followed her into the room. One or two heads looked up as they both wove their way past their desks. As they neared the end of the office, where the conference table stood, a tall thin young man approached them holding out a file.

'Hey boss how was your meeting? This is the missing file you were looking for yesterday, it had got mixed up with some completed stuff ready for filing.'

The woman didn't make eye contact with him but took the file and continued on through the room saying.

'Not good enough sergeant, if we'd lost it then zis mornings meeting would 'ave been pointless. You need to sharpen up, OUI!'

'Yes boss, sorry.'

She glanced over her shoulder at the man and nodded as if to make her point. Reaching the large table she threw the illusive file onto one of the piles of papers, slipped off her jacket hanging it on the back of a chair and turned to Nita indicating for her to sit.

'I think we 'ave to introduce ourselves now don't you? I'm Inspector Miriam Dubois of the Police National, I was based in Paris until seconded 'ere to work wis Superintendent Allen in zis new unit primarily tracking and prosecuting gangs trafficking young women and girls throughout Europe and the UK for sex and prostitution. My guess is you are ze young lady detective he talks so highly of?'

Nita smiled and nodded, even before the inspector had introduced herself she'd detected her French accent.

'Mam yes, I'm Detective Constable Nita Patel, I'm one of the detectives based at Portbridge and worked with Superintendent Allen on a particularly nasty case.'

The inspector nodded then said.

'Before we go any further Nita, can l call you Nita?'

She nodded.

'So, I am sad for your loss Nita, DS Allen 'as outlined what happened l cannot begin to understand how hard things are for you just now but if you decide to join us zen I'm always 'ere to speak wis you or just to listen. Do you understand?'

'Thank you mam yes l understand. Can l ask, does everyone here know what has happened?'

'Officially no we 'ave not said anything to the section but no doubt, as you know things could 'ave been heard from other sources or work colleagues.'

Nita smiled slightly knowing only too well how 'scuttle-butt,' Chinese whispers spread. Miriam glanced over her shoulder then back at her, pushed her chair back and stood up. Nita turned to see who the inspector had seen and saw DS Allen walking through the office. Holding his hand out as he neared the long table, he smiled broadly, Nita stood.

'Nita, DC Patel,' he said shaking her hand, 'I'm really pleased you decided to come up and see us and what inspector Dubois and I are trying to set up here.'

He sat down on a chair between the inspector and Nita and continued.

'l have to say you look very well considering all you've been through, how are you fitting in at the office?'

'Thank sir, yes okay it's good to be back and working with DS Syms again,'

'Are they looking after you?'

'They are thank you being involved has helped me a lot, it's been a good distraction. I'm still having some counselling but not as often, in a sense work is providing the same therapy to be honest.'

'Good, good.' he said nodding. 'Now, you two have obviously introduced yourselves, I'm sorry I wasn't here to meet you but the inspector and I got tied up at a strategy meeting this morning.'

The inspector passed him the file she'd been given when Nita and she had walked through the office earlier. He glanced at her and held the file up a little, his expression asking a question. She shook her head slightly saying,

'It got mixed up wis some other files by accident.'

'Mmm, not good enough Miriam, that could have lost us the evidence you know, they'll need to be more careful where stuff is, I'll mention it at Monday's briefing.'

Looking at Nita briefly he smiled, adding. 'Remember those Mondays detective?'

She grinned, 'Oh yes sir too well, Ruth, I mean inspector Dodd's still holds them.'

'Glad to hear it, to my mind it focus's everyone's attention after the weekend break don't you think?

He glanced at both women briefly.

'Right, so here we are, we're newly formed with officers from all over Europe as part of the team; some of whom were involved with you in our case. You've got an idea what we are trying to do and I would like… no, I want you here with us because you had such an input back then. How do you feel about joining us?'

'Erm, well l was surprised sir when Ruth, inspector Dodd's spoke to me about this. It's 6 years since 'Operation Hawkeye' and I've not had any direct involvement in any similar cases since then so I'm wondering why you want me on the team.?'

Over the next hour the Superintendent and inspector talked to Nita about the aims and objectives of this internationally staffed unit working cases involving all forms of trafficking. They invited her to join them for lunch and as they made their way to the restaurant, introduced her to a couple of other detectives who she sat with. She realised they'd been briefed to talk with her and answer any questions about how all the case evidence was collected and processed. For a brief time in the afternoon she shadowed one of them before a final talk with DS Allen and Inspector Miriam Dubois. Finally winding up the meeting they stood together around the long table, the Superintendent shook Nita's hand.

'Think about what we've said today and what you've seen and learned. I don't want you to feel I'm putting pressure on you to join us Nita but l know how you work, how thorough you are and l reckon you'd be a real asset here.' Glancing at the inspector he added, 'If you're not sure about something or feel you'd like more information I'm sure inspector Dubois would be happy to talk things through with you.'

The inspector nodded, 'I am 'ere if you want to speak wis me, like l said zis morning, call me anytime okay.' She shook Nita's hand, 'Au revoir detective it 'as been nice to meet you, zis lady Superintendent Allen speaks so much about! I would be very 'appy should you come and be part of zis unit.'

'Thank you mam, sir, I've a lot to think about over the weekend.'

'Yes, but I need your answer soon Nita… soon please,' he replied.

'Yes sir.'

With that she left returning home to Portbridge, her head full of questions.

Late Monday morning she walked into the office, said hello to Alan, Linda and one or two others before knocking on Ruth's door frame. She was on the phone but looked up beckoning her to come in then held up her mug. Nita took the mug nodded and went off returning a couple of minutes later with two drinks. Ruth replaced the phone as she came back into the office.

'Morning how are you today?'

'Yes, good thanks boss, spent most of the weekend mulling over Friday's meeting.'

'Have you decided then?'

'I've got a lot of questions I'm still asking myself, it's a huge step up from working here with you and everyone, we're all sort of family you know. Up there it's definitely big time you know, international stuff, it's like they're an off shoot of Interpol. Right now boss I don't know that I want to be part of that.'

Ruth shrugged sucking air in through her teeth and grimaced slightly.

'Oh dear, someone's going to be disappointed then, they've talked you up to do the job.'

In silence she studied Nita on the other side of the desk and after a few moments leaned towards her saying quietly.

'Nita lovie I don't think you've given yourself enough time to have thought this through properly. Listen you've got a bit of accrued time to take back, can I suggest you go and think about it?'

Nita grinned. 'Funny you should say that 'cause that was going to be the second part of me being here this morning. There's something I need to sort out, just family stuff you know but I need to go and talk to Emma face to face.'

'Perfect… bugger off then and sort it, you've got until next Monday's briefing. I'll fend off any awkward questions until then, will that help?'

She grinned again. 'You're an absolute star boss, thank you. I've got a counselling session tomorrow morning then I'll go down to Bristol, thank you.'

She got to the door when Ruth said.

'By the way the inspector, Miriam what's-her-name, liked you!'

Nita looked back at her quizzically, Ruth nodded.

'Thought you had the right attitude.' she added.

Walking back through the office she touched Alan Syms' shoulder as she passed his desk.

'Taking a few days to do some thinking, see you next Monday okay.'

He glanced at her, nodded and winked.

'No problem, hope you get it sorted, take care, be safe.'

She waved closing the office door behind her.

Chapter Ten

Leaving Portbridge just after lunch the following day, she drove the 200 miles to Bristol arriving around seven in the evening. Greeted at the door by Angus he held his finger to his lips to keep her quiet.

'Emma's just settling them down,' he said, 'we haven't told them you're coming tonight, we didn't want them to get silly and then not sleep.'

'Fine,' she whispered back. 'that means I'll get some sleep before the onslaught tomorrow then.'

He grinned at her.

'Leave your bags for now we'll get them later.'

Following him into the house they went through to the kitchen and sat waiting for Emma to join them.

'Something smells nice,' she said, 'I've just realised how hungry l am.'

'Emma's tried to follow one of your curry dishes, we have it, well her version of it quite often.'

Emma eventually came through and the two of them embraced for some time.

'How are you?' she asked, 'Good journey?'

'I'm good thanks, yes good journey steady away just about four hours; how are the twins?'

Emma smiled, 'Asleep… they'll be so surprised to see you here in the morning.'

She glanced at Angus.

'We thought it best not to say anything tonight, they'd get too excited and giddy and we weren't sure how you'd be after the drive down.'

While the two had been talking Angus brought a bottle of wine and some glasses into the kitchen. Emma moved to a simmering pan on the cooker giving the contents a stir; glancing over her shoulder at Nita she said.

'This is one of your curries, well as near as l can get it to yours it's one we like and it's easy, is that alright for you?'

Nita shrugged and grinned.

'Fine by me, Louise won't do one when I'm there, she's worried I'll say something about how she's prepared it.' They both giggled.

After the meal they went and sat in the lounge talking about how they were both coping with the process of getting their lives back together. Nita told them about being back at work and the possible move to the new unit expressing some of her reservations to them. With the girls at home and work supporting her she was sleeping much better, she felt being back at work was contributing to fewer meltdowns. Emma agreed saying that having the twins meant there wasn't the time to dwell on things. Sometimes in an evening if Angus was working late or at some function she'd catch herself having one of those 'moments.' They both said the evenings were the worst remembering it was then Stephen used to call them particularly when he was on the Scandinavian runs. Just before eleven they turned in for the night after Nita had briefly explained Robert Grahams call about *Finbar* and the fact that they needed to talk about what they should do with her.

Around seven the following morning the sounds of children rushing about brought Nita out of a long peaceful sleep. Stretching she listened to the chatter and activity downstairs punctuated occasionally by either Emma or Angus cautioning one or both the twins to calm down. Pulling her dressing gown from her case she pulled it on and slipping her feet into her slippers opened her door and started down the stairs, the fourth and fifth steps creaked and she heard Emma say.

'Oh, sounds like there's someone on our stairs, l wonder who that might be.'

Moments later two little faces appeared at the foot of the stairs. Taken a little by surprise at Nita's appearance the twins stood and stared for a few moments then came the realisation who she was. Almost together they exclaimed excitedly.

'Nani, Nani.'

Elizabeth dashed back to the kitchen shouting.

'Mummy mummy Nani's here, she on the stairs.'

Rory stood and waited until she was sitting on the step then he climbed onto her lap hugging her.

'Nani, I've missed you.' he said squeezing her.

Elizabeth was back now dragging Emma with her.

'Look mummy it's Nani she's here, she must have come in when we were all asleep.'

She climbed onto Nita's lap now and hugged and kissed her, Emma giggled at the sight but saw Nita's eyes were full of tears.

'Come on you two,' she said softly to them, 'let Nani get up and come and sit with us while you both finish your toast.'

It was Nita's turn now to be half dragged into the kitchen. Sitting opposite them at the bar Emma put a mug of tea in front of her while she cut the children's toast into fingers. Stroking her shoulder briefly Emma said quietly.

'Are you okay, I'm sorry but they can be a bit full on in the morning; you were near to tears just now?'

Putting a hand over Emma's on her shoulder she looked at her.

'Mmmm yes, Rory said he'd missed me, it was so sweet l just choked a little.'

Angus appeared in the kitchen doorway dressed smartly in a two-piece grey suit, blue shirt and contrasting tie. Elizabeth went to get down from her bar chair but Emma coughed.

'No Miss, you stay there!'

Pouting, she pulled a long face but responded when Emma said.

'You can tell daddy from there.'

Instantly she perked up saying.

'Look daddy Nani's here, she must have come when we were all asleep.'

Kissing Emma's proffered cheek he passed onto Nita and kissed hers' then looking at Elizabeth said.

'Well, what a surprise,' then winking at Nita said, 'I must have forgotten to lock the door last night, naughty daddy aye?'

Both children responded.

'Naughty daddy you left the door open.' Rory added straight away, 'If it had been locked then Nani would have had to sleep in the car like you did once daddy.'

Nita looked at Angus then Emma quizzically, 'Oh yes?'

Angus put his finger to his lips looking at Rory, 'Shhhh…'

Emma laughed.

'He'd been to a 'men only' staff do, I'd had a,' she gave a little cough, 'glass of wine and went to bed before he got home and erm… locked the doors. Poor daddy couldn't make me hear so spent the night in the car in the garage!!'

Nita looked at them again laughing.

'Out of the mouths of babes, hhmm.'

'I made it up to him later.'

She exchanged a knowing glance with him, they both smiled, Nita said quietly.

'Okay TMI 'nough said!'

Turning to the twins Nita said.

'I thought I'd just pop down to see you both because I've missed you soooo much. You know Nani is a police detective?'

They both stared at her listening intently.

'Well we detectives have this special key that opens any door we need to, so l used that to get in last night and sneaked up to bed.'

Angus said, 'Do you think Nani could get me one?'

The three of them laughed; walking around the bar he encircled Emma's waist kissing her neck and cheek.

'Right weans daddy's off to work.' He moved to kiss them both. 'What's daddy doing?'

Together they shouted, 'Daddy's AWA ta work!'

He grinned as he walked to the front door.

'See you lovely ladies around sixish hopefully, bye.'

'Right.' Emma said exhaling as the door closed, 'Let's get some order in here, now my little cherubs it's Wednesday so we are off to mother and toddler at the church okay?'

This news was greeted by shrieks and whoops from them, Emma laughed beginning to explain to Nita.

'There's a group of us meet at church, we call it the 'Crèche in the Crypt' The children love it they get to mix with others and as they play learn to share do you want to come?'

'Why not.' Nita replied.

Turning to Rory and Elizabeth Emma said quietly.

'Nani wants to come with us, is that okay?'

Both children nodded enthusiastically.

'So let's get dressed and get our stuff together.'

Arriving at the church at the same time as a couple of other mothers, they and their respective gaggle of chattering children trooped into the building and joined half a dozen other parents already there. There was an assortment of big toys and blocks scattered around a carpeted open area at the back of the church. The new arrivals just dived into the area joining the children already playing. Off to one side a trellis table was set up with juice and biscuits on it and behind that a small table with an electric earn steaming away and around it milk, tea and coffee pots and cups. Emma introduced Nita to some of the mums, the vicar and his assistant as they took a cup of tea from the table. Nita sat off to one side watching the twins mixing with the other children. The lady helping the vicar came to sit with her.

'You've come with Emma and the twins am I right?'

Nita nodded, 'Yes she's sort of my daughter-in-law, I was her father's partner.'

'Ahh okay, I'm Amanda by the way.' They shook hands and Amanda said, 'Can I say how sorry I am for your loss it was such a tragic accident. Our group of mums' tried to be as supportive for Emma as we could be, she's really quite remarkable; to have lost her mother so young and now her dad, so hard so devastating I'm sorry, how are you holding up with all this?'

'Oh you know, day by day, we speak to each other every day and share stuff. Emma has Angus and the twins and I can see now all the support she has here.'

Amanda looked around the room.

'Yes, our little community is very close we are always there for anyone who needs a prayer or a shoulder. It works you know, the vicar is wonderful at knowing just what to say when it matters, do you have some support at home?'

Nita nodded.

'I have yes, I shared a house with a couple of girls before I met Stephen and they've just been a god-send. I don't know if Emma has said, but I'm a police officer so work have made the force support network available for me, at the end of the day even with all the help in the world, I know how I'm suffering and equally how Emma is too. Everyone says it gets easier with time but from where I am right now it doesn't look that way to me!'

Amanda took hold of Nita's hand, gently squeezing it.

'I don't want to preach but prayer can be really comforting and strengthening.' She smiled and shrugged a little, 'I'm not saying it has to be, Our Father or Dear Lord… but just to talk honestly, out loud, can be very uplifting.'

Nita looked at the woman's hand holding hers then into her eyes, she was smiling at her softly and nodding, she felt a sudden rush of emotion and welled up. She tried to say something but no words came as this surge of emotion threatened to overwhelm her. Amanda, still watching her moved a little closer still holding her hand.

'Nita it's fine honestly, just let yourself go don't fight this relax into it and let go.'

Sensing she was losing control she wanted this sudden rush of emotion to stop but was still unable to speak. Inside she felt this overwhelming sense of being lost in a vast place, looking forlornly at Amanda she couldn't fight it anymore and just submitted to the feelings. Relaxing against Amanda she wasn't crying but there were tears just flowing down her cheeks. Amanda took her in her arms holding her for a long time until she said softly beside Nita's head.

'Nita these tears are healing tears, it's your mind and body releasing all the pain and grief you've locked away to protect yourself. It's important you let it go or it will slow your recovery and stop you moving forward.'

They sat together like this for what seemed ages to Nita but she really did began to feel easier in herself and realised the tears had stopped. She felt a sense of peace deep inside something she hadn't felt since Stephen had left on that last trip. Gently she pushed herself up breaking away from Amanda. Taking some tissues from her bag she dabbed her cheeks smiling at the woman feeling a little embarrassed by what had just happened, Amanda returned her smile and stroking her thigh said quietly.

'To cry or rant is not showing a weakness you know. Okay, you have Emma and your network of friends and colleagues at home to talk to but in the middle of the night when you're alone and your head is all over the place let that emotion go. Just like you have this morning and remember these are healing tears, simply talk to God. He says come unto me all who are heavy laden and I will give you rest, you'll be surprised how much better you'll feel when that moment has passed. Now are you alright, would you like a cup of tea?'

Nita took a deep breath, puffing up her cheeks then exhaling.

'Ohh please l feel I've just… well l don't know what l feel to be honest but a cup of tea would be perfect.'

Amanda returned a few minutes later and stayed with Nita until everyone began clearing the toys and things away. They talked about Nita's job, Amanda was surprised that she'd spent time with a Police force in America, laughing at some of the funny excuses people gave when they have been caught 'red-handed'. Nita said good-bye to some of the other mum's then with Emma and the twins spent a few moments talking to the vicar with Amanda by his side. As they left the hall Amanda hugged her.

'Come and see us again, you're most welcome to join us at service if you are so inclined just speak to Emma, she comes and joins us sometimes. Take care Nita, l hope you feel more at peace, it's been lovely to meet you.'

Nita smiled, 'Thank you, you have helped to make this massive cloud disappear l feel so much brighter in myself.'

With everyone in the car they waved to the vicar and Amanda at the hall doorway as they set off home. There wasn't much conversation on the journey except for the twins chattering away until they both fell asleep. Emma glanced at Nita a couple of times and smiled, she looked to be asleep too.

Evening meal finished and the twins bathed read to and settled for the night, the three of them settled in the living room with the remnants of the bottle of wine they'd opened to accompany their dinner.

'So did you girls have a good day together?' Angus asked.

They glanced at each other and Emma replied.

'Well I was chatting to some of the other mums and watching the twins playing, but this one,' she said nodding towards Nita, 'was in deep conversation with Amanda.'

Nita nodded and said quietly.

'We were just talking about things you know, she was asking me about what I did, then how was I managing with everything you know.'

Emma was watching her.

'My guess is,' she said 'she gave you a different perspective on coping with dad's accident, yes?'

She nodded again thoughtfully.

'Yes, just what's her job at the church?'

'She's a Deacon at the church and she works with Cruise as well.' Emma replied, 'She helped me so much after the accident and later after the funeral, she was just amazing at helping me through each day.'

It was Emma's turn to pause and remember back just 5 months. After a few moments reflection she looked at Nita and continued.

'It was like she could see into me, into my soul, she knew just what to say every time. It was like she touched a nerve and saw me beginning to get emotional then put it right in a few words, do you understand?'

Nita nodded slowly, adding.

'Exactly I felt that too Em, I could have burst into tears at one point… in fact I did… she just held my hand and spoke so quietly to me and I felt strong… not the wreck I've been, I felt safe. Do you think she's had a similar loss sometime?'

Emma shrugged.

'Don't know, I've never heard anything, she's always around and I know other mum's have spent time talking to her.'

Angus shared the remaining wine between them and sat next to Emma. Taking her hand he looked across to Nita.

'Can we talk about the elephant in the room now? You said you wanted to speak about *Finbar.*'

She nodded.

'Yes, Robert called last week wanting to know what to do about *Finbar.* She's out of the water and he's asking if there's anything we want doing service wise.'

Emma glanced at Angus then Nita.

'Yes, I'd forgotten I spoke to Robert around the time of the memorial service and said I'd be in touch when things had settled. What are we going to do with the boat?'

They talked through all sorts of options until quite late and decided to think about it again in the morning.

Bright and early Nita was woken by two little children landing on her bed and smothering her with kisses. She was finally rescued by Emma who called the twins to calm down and go downstairs for their breakfasts.

'Listen you two terrors… let Nani wake up and she will come down to sit with you. Now go …shooo.'

She smiled as she followed the twins out of the room closing the door, saying.

'There will be a cafetiere of coffee waiting for you when you're ready.'

A short time later Nita walked into the kitchen immediately being badgered to sit between the children, Angus grinned broadly.

'Oh you are going to need that coffee you'll be mythered to within an inch of your life by the time I get home tonight, better you than me. Right, daddy's…'

The sentence was finished loudly by the twins, 'Awa ta work!'

He kissed Emma's proffered cheek then the twins and finally Nita saying quietly in her ear.

'Good luck Nani, have a nice day.'

As Emma began to clear away the dishes Elizabeth and Rory went off to play in their den while Nita stayed at the breakfast bar with her coffee.'

'Right I need to do the supermarket this morning, do you want some peace or to come and join us. I must warn you it can get quite intense sometimes.' Emma said.

Nita thought for a moment.

'If it's alright with you I'll stay I have to work through some stuff of my own really.'

'About the job, the options?'

'Yeah.'

'If you need a sound board I'm happy to listen when we get back.'

She smiled at Emma.

'That might be good actually, thanks.'

Emma gently stroked her shoulder as she passed by her, calling.

'Come on you two monkey's shoes and coats, we're going shopping.'

A few minutes later Nita was sitting alone listening to the peace of the house she smiled, it was a lovely house very modern open and bright, she sensed the atmosphere it felt a happy place. Moving to the living room she sat, took a notepad from her bag and looked at the list of points she'd written down to remind herself why she was here and what she needed to do. By the time Emma returned from the shopping spree, laden with bags Nita had pretty much decided what she wanted to do ticking some points she'd made, scoring through others she wasn't happy about.

When Emma barged and crashed through the door with the bags and the twins excitedly pushing past her to tell Nita what they'd done and that they had a surprise for her, she felt good about finally deciding what she would tell Ruth on Monday morning. She sighed and went to help Emma sort and put away the mountain of tins, fresh and frozen vegetables and fruit. With the kitchen clear and tidy, she made a pot of tea for the two of them and some fruit juice for the children. Emma called them before sitting at the breakfast bar.

'What have you done with Nani's surprise?'

The two children walked into the kitchen looking very sheepish, Nita and Emma exchanged a quick glance before Emma said.

'Okay, what have you done, where's the box?'

Elizabeth immediately said.

'It was Rory mummy!'

He responded instantly.

'It wasn't me… it was Lizzy, she opened it.'…

'NO it wasn't, you did'

Suddenly both children were crying. Nita walked around the breakfast bar and taking each child by the hand led them out of the kitchen into the living room. Sitting on the settee she looked at the two forlorn, tearful faces watching her.

'Hhhmmm, what are we going to do about this then, I think we need to see the evidence don't you?'

Elizabeth go and fetch the box for me please.'

As the little girl went away Nita noticed Emma watching from the edge of the kitchen door, she smiled giving the slightest of a nod. Rory started to speak, Nita put a finger to his lips.

'Wait!'

Elizabeth came back into the room holding an expensive looking cake box handing it to Nita and began to say.

'Nani, it…'

She did the same to her as she'd done to Rory.

'Wait here you two.' she said.

Going into the kitchen, leaving the twins standing by the settee, Emma came and looked over her shoulder to see two empty trays where cakes had been and of the four remaining cakes, two had teeth marks in them and were missing corners, Emma spluttered quietly.

'Little monkeys.' she said.

Nita smiled, 'If they've being naughty what do you do?'

'They sit on the naughty step for a bit, why?'

Nita nodded, 'Okay.'

She returned to the living room with the box to the where the twins were still standing. Sitting again she opened the box and showed Elizabeth and Rory where the missing cakes had been and where two tiny bites had been taken from the other cakes Rory sobbed, Elizabeth cried quietly.

'Now listen to me!' Nita said firmly.

The twins had never heard 'Nani' speak with such authority in her voice.

'There is the evidence, yes? Two cakes have gone and two cakes have little teeth marks in them. I'm not going to ask who did what but I am going to ask why? You both knew we were going to have cakes soon so why did you steal yours first and nibble two more…hhhmmm?'

The twins just stood there in front of Nita struck dumb.

'Anything to say… NO… okay. So when you're naughty for mummy or daddy what happens?'

Rory began to mumble, Nita waited then said.

'Tell me again Rory but this time don't mumble… alright.'

'Mummy makes us sit on the naughty step.'

'Okay,' Nita said, 'so first, I think you need to go and say sorry to mummy, she's upset that the two of you spoiled the surprise. When you've done that come back here to me.'

The pair walked away to the kitchen where she heard the children talking to Emma amid little chokes and sobs, a few minutes later they came back holding Emma's hand.

'I think we need to say sorry to Nani, don't you?'

'Sorry for taking the cakes Nani we won't do it again… promise.'

Nita nodded holding up a little finger.

'Will that be a 'pinkie promise' because that's a true promise not to be broken… ever!'

The twins nodded and linked their little fingers with Nita's. They grinned broadly for a moment until Emma added.

'Go to the den and bring your chairs here and sit on them until I say you can move.'

Very sheepishly the pair went and fetched their little chairs into the living room where Emma placed them in different corners and sat them down. Emma and Nita talked about the shopping trip then how Nita had got on making her decision about the job offer. For quite some time the twins sat quietly, eventually beginning to fidget. Emma looked at the clock then Nita saying.

'Fancy an omelette for lunch.'

'Oh yes, that would be fine.'

Then to the twins.

'Would you two like a boiled egg with soldiers?'

In fifteen minutes or so the four of them were sitting at the breakfast bar enjoying their lunches. The twins remained quiet and subdued through the afternoon until Angus arrived home. He was a little surprised to see they were in their pyjamas but guessed that there must have been an issue, they seemed quite happy but he sensed an air of tension.

'Hello everyone, this is a bit of surprise you two ready for bed, does someone want to tell me what has happened?'

Elizabeth and Rory each began to tell of the earlier event blaming the other sibling. Quickly, amidst the verbal onslaught he held his hand up to quieten them.

'Tell you what, I'll go and speak to a detective and find out exactly what happened. You two sit quietly until I come back, okay?'

The children sat back again turning their attention back to the cartoon they'd been watching on the television. Finding the two women sitting in the kitchen with a glass of wine each he grinned and kissed Emma.

'Well whatever happened must have been pretty momentous?'

Between them, Emma and Nita relayed the mornings events to him trying to maintain an air of shock and displeasure in case the twins could overhear their conversation, whilst what they wanted to do was laugh at the whole scenario especially the part where 'Nani' interviewed them in her best detective persona. Explanation complete Angus thought about what to do for a few moments before saying to them.

'We need to end this in such a way that the 'monkey's' don't go to bed still up-set and have bad dreams. Have they said they're sorry to you?'

'Oh yes, to both of us.' Emma said.

'Right, will you do their bedtime drinks whilst I have a word with them,' looking at Nita he said, 'will you come with me.'

Emma began to make the drinks for the twins whilst Angus with Nita joined the twins in the living room. They sat on the settee and looked at the children.

'So what are we to do about this then you two?' Angus said.

Elizabeth and Rory returned their look sheepishly, Rory began to say.

'It was Lizzy daddy, she said we…'

Angus held his hand up and the boy fell silent.

'Wheest,' he said then quietly and calmly continued, 'we all know what happened, the question is what are we going to do about it? It was a treat because Nani was here, you both know it was wrong to take your cake first before you all sat down just so you got the one you wanted. Do you not think mummy and Nani would have asked you, given you a choice to pick one? I'm very disappointed, we are all disappointed. Mummy and I have always shared with you both, yes?'

The two children nodded. Angus remained quiet for a while hopefully to let his words sink in.

'Right, now I know you've already apologised to mummy and Nani, but I want to hear you say to them that you won't ever do this again, alright.'

At that point Emma came into the living room with a tray of drinks. Putting them on the coffee table in the centre of the room she sat next to Nita and looked at the twins. They got off their chairs and came to stand in front of the two women. Rory began first followed by Elizabeth like an echo, their voices, interspersed with shallow sobs, so quiet that Angus said they'd have to say everything again this time so they could all hear. Having said their piece again they stood very forlorn waiting for a response from the three adults. Nita reached out and took each of the children by their hand drawing them towards her and cuddled them close to her.

'Thank you for that, we still love you you know but you should have known mummy and I would have shared the treat with you.' She kissed both the children and squeezed them adding, 'Go and give mummy a big hug and get your drinks and I think; mummy and daddy, we can consider this matter closed don't you agree?'

The twins went to Emma and she took them in her arms, kissed them saying.

'I think so, I hope you've both realised that sharing things is a lot nicer than just helping yourself, yes?'

The children nodded as Emma passed them their drinks. Angus shuffled away from Emma a little and said.

'Don't I get a cuddle aye?'

The two children moved to sit either side of him and he drew them close under each arm and they snuggle tightly into his side. They all sat quietly as the children drank their drinks and as they finished Emma said softly.

'Come on you two, teeth toilet and stories, say night night.'

The twins kissed Angus and went to Nita. Hugging them she looked at Emma.

'Do you think Nani can read the story tonight?'

'Why not, would you like that?' Emma said.

'Yes, yes please Nani.'

The children jumped about excitedly as Emma and Nita lead the way to bed. At the living room door Emma looked back at Angus and mimed drinking from a glass, grinning at her he nodded. Finally with the children settled asleep, the three of them sat together sampling one of Angus's 'special reds', he felt they deserved it after today's traumas! They talked once more through their final plans about what they were going to do with *Finbar.* They were each concerned that the three of them were in absolute agreement and not feeling pressured. Sitting forward on the settee Angus said.

'Right, for the last time then we are going to ask Mr G to find a broker for us and put the boat on the market… last time yes!'

Emma and Nita nodded, Angus looked from one to the other.

'It's up to you two, Emma you've so much invested in her and she was your safe place for so long. Nita your time with Stephen centred round her, so you have to be sure here.'

Both the women nodded, Emma said.

'It's true but we have to move on and it would be a travesty to just leave her in the Grahams yard or anyone else's for that matter just gathering rust and quietly rotting. Look over the past few years well since we've had the twins really, all we've done, the family's done, is a bit of cruising around the coast. She could give another family the same pleasure we've all had from her over the years. I know it sounds a bit silly but she's sort of family and deservers a better future than just falling apart somewhere.'

She looked at Angus then Nita and shrugged, 'Sorry.'

Nita reached across for her hand and squeezed it, with tears in her eyes she said.

'Just how I feel Em, took the words out of my mouth.'

'Okay, who's going to speak to Mr G then?' Angus said.

'I can go up to the yard and see him or do you want to call him?'

Nita said, Emma shook her head.

'No I'll call him first I think then if he finds somewhere to offer her maybe you could go and talk to him, is that alright?'

'Yes fine by me just keep me in the loop.'

'Okay,' Angus said, 'Now let's get down to you, have you decided what you're going to do yet?'

Nita smiled, 'I think so, the offer's great, I mean to work with an international team on something I was basically in on the ground floor with would be amazing but I think I'm going to stay where I am at Portbridge.'

'Okay.' Angus said grinning, 'Final answer!'

The three of them laughed as Nita nodded in reply.

'Final answer.'

'Right so we've sorted out all the business in hand,' Angus said, 'tomorrow's the weekend, now not wanting to get rid of you or anything like that, have you any plans about going home or are we all together for the weekend?'

They sat and talked through ideas for the weekend settling on a Saturday wandering around the historic maritime places of interest around Bristol and asking if their regular babysitter Jess was available

Saturday evening so the three of them could go out. During this conversation Nita decided she'd set off back to Portbridge after lunch on Sunday so she was ready to see the 'boss' Monday morning with her decision about the new job. All in all the weekend worked out pretty much as planned except for the evening out However, not all was lost, Angus cooked for the three of them and to be honest they enjoyed the evening, the food and wines just as much as they would had they gone to a restaurant. Sunday began quiet and peaceful but as the time came for Nita to set off back to Portbridge following a light lunch the mood changed becoming a little sombre. Taking the twins in her arms she kissed and cuddled them tightly then turned her attention to Emma. No words were spoken as they embraced for some time but they both had tears in their eyes as they separated, Emma letting her arm slip off NIta's affectionately as she walked towards her car. Angus hugged her, as she kissed his cheek she said softly.

'Look after her… yes?'

He nodded, 'I will and you take care, stay strong! Nita, call if it's getting tough again, we will come up.'

She nodded and turned away to get into her car but he held onto her arm firmly.

'That should have been yes Angus! I mean it Nita, call!'

She looked down at his hand on her arm, nodded once more and replied with a slight smile.

'Hhmm, yes Angus, thank you.'

He released her arm and she settled in the driving seat, he closed the door. As she moved off the driveway the twins were jumping up and down excitedly frantically waving as both Emma and Angus shouted, 'Call when you're home.'

Waving out of the driver's window she tooted the horn, pulled out onto the main road heading towards the M5 and home. As the evening sun set over the more familiar horizon and outlines of the buildings of Portbridge Nita finally emptied the last bits from her car, made a pot of tea, settled in the cosy living room and called Emma and Angus. Sitting a little while later she realised that coming back to the little terraced house after being away for a break was becoming less traumatic. She was beginning to feel comfortable again, less emotional. She smiled, and even happier that she'd made her decision about the changing jobs or not. Altogether content in herself she locked up and weary from the days' drive went to bed.

Chapter Eleven

Arriving at the office in time to hear all the progress reports from the different teams at the Monday briefing Nita sat at her desk. Standing beside the Inspector, Alan Syms nodded to her as Ruth questioned different detectives and gave updates on any external developments linked to any of the various on-going cases. As she brought the meeting to an end she looked directly at Nita then her office. Nita acknowledged her as the Inspector concluded the meeting.

'Right everyone lets go and catch some criminals,' raising her voice a little she added, 'BUT be careful and stay safe okay, go!'

The meeting broke up as Nita went towards Ruth's office, passing Alan, he grinned at her.

'Good few days away, did you get stuff sorted?'

'Yeah thanks, all very productive and spending time with Emma has helped us both find some perspective l think, overall l feel in a good place right now.'

Alan nodded. 'Good.'

She touched his arm.

'A lot of this is down to you, the boss, Lou and Moira too you know.'

He smiled, 'The boss will be pleased to see you back.'

Nita knocked on the frame of the door, without looking up from some paper she was studying, the inspector held her mug up. Nita turned and brewed two teas for them and joined her in her office.

'Morning good few days?'

'Yeah thank you boss. I've just been saying to Alan, spending time with Emma has helped us both focus on moving on, it's certainly helped me make my mind up about this post they've offered me. I think for the first time since the accident I feel really okay in myself. Am I making sense here?'

All this time the inspector, Ruth, had been watching her looking for something that said I'm better.

'Well let me tell you detective this is the first time in a long time you've come across as the Nita I knew; that's good to hear. Now I've been batting for you here lovie, am I glad you're back 'cause the phone's been ringing off the hook from division.'

Leaning forward across her desk she looked into Nita's eyes intently saying quietly but with an air of authority.

'I just hope you've made the right decision detective or our lives could get very messy, if you know what I mean!'

Nita squirmed a little under such scrutiny but replied.

'I've spent most of the weekend thinking about it and finally decided I want to stay… here… Right answer boss?'

'NO… it's bloody not!... Ohh my god the shit's going to hit the fan now!'

Ruth jumped up from her seat, making Nita sit back into her chair and began pacing round her little office.

'Honestly Nita, for me and us here in Portbridge that's great news but the DI's going to be hell to work with. He really thought you'd jump at the idea of joining his new squad… bloody hell I did not expect that decision!'

Ruth's outburst had been so loud and unexpected that besides shocking Nita a little, one or two heads of other detective in the office looked around to see what the raised voice was all about. Ruth stopped pacing and turned to Nita.

'Sorry about that Nita but I genuinely did not expect you to throw that chance out of the window.'

Sitting again she studied Nita for some time who shuffled quite a bit, conscious of being under such scrutiny.

'Why… why did you decide to turn that down and stay? Oh don't get me wrong lovie… I'm glad you're staying, this might sound mercenary but still having you as part of our team means we stand a fair chance of keeping our conviction rate up.'

'Honestly boss, at first I was really tempted, it sort of felt that all we did on 'Hawkeye' was finally being appreciated. Then I started to think it's almost seven years since 'Hawkeye' and so much has changed regarding how we're working to fight the trafficking gangs. It's all got so technical I mean the unit at division is really amazing, it's all so high tech and all the other European units are linked in, plus there's even a drone section. The other thing is apart from the French inspector and the Super I'd be the granny. I seriously thought about it then went away this weekend and talking to Emma finally decided I'd stay here… and make your life hell! No… I realised that I'm an old fashioned grass roots detective.'

She giggled as she said this then laughed when she saw the look Ruth gave her then said.

'Am I going to tell him or are you?'

'Me… not on your life lovie, that's down to you and by the way you've got a meeting with him and the inspector 10am Wednesday at division.'

'What! Seriously Wednesday.'

The inspector nodded slowly, deliberately, grinning at Nita.

'Good luck with that detective now, there's work to be done here, so sod off and find Alan.'

Over the next couple of days Alan Syms brought her up to speed with their ongoing cases.

Wednesday morning, Nita travelled to Divisional HQ for her meeting with Superintendent Allen and the inspector Miriam Dubois. Feeling quite apprehensive about how they would respond to her decision to remain at Portbridge she waited to meet them.

'Nita Patel?'

A lady's voice made her jump, she turned to see a uniformed constable just outside a nearby door.

'Would you come in please?'

She stood and followed the constable into a small wood panelled office where the Superintendent and the inspector sat at a desk. Superintendent Allen stood and shook her hand.

'Good morning detective I hope you are managing to continue your recovery.'

'Morning sir, morning ma'am,' she acknowledged the inspector, 'Yes sir thank you, I've just spent some time with Stephens's daughter Emma and I think that has helped to put things into perspective. We both felt more positive by the end of the weekend and ready to begin to move forward and rebuild our lives again.'

'Good, I'm really pleased to hear that and you know, of course that you can still use our counselling team if needs be.'

'Yes sir thank you.'

The group settled down and the constable having served everyone with drinks left the room.

It was almost an hour before the three of them emerged from the office, Superintendent Allan shook Nita's hand and walked off along the corridor. The inspector shook her hand but kept hold of it.

'If in ze next two weeks or so you 'ave a change of hart and feel you would like to join us, call me. I'm sure something can be arranged and you will still be able to come 'ere detective. I know ze Superintendent is disappointed by your decision,' she grinned, 'Ee was sure you would be coming 'ere, but l understand what you said about being a grass roots detective. Yes it is very high tech now but we 'ave to try and stay ahead of ze's gangs, you know what it is like, you read it in ze papers. It 'as been a pleasure to have met you detective and put a face to a celebrity, good luck for ze future.'

Nita chuckled and replied.

'Oh I'm not sure about the celebrity bit ma'am, but it has been lovely to meet you and see how original 'Operation Hawkeye' has advanced.'

The inspector nodded 'Oui bon' au revoir detective.'

The two women set off along the corridor in different directions and just after 2'o'clock Nita walked into the office in Portbridge and straight into her inspectors room. Sitting back in her chair she studied Nita for a few moments.

'Well how was it?'

'Okay but he's not a happy duck. I'm glad the inspector was there too, it could have got awkward if it had just been the two of us.'

'Am l going to catch a load of flack?'

'Don't think so, he just walked away a bit huffy but the inspector spoke to me and said she understood why I'd turned it down. She's okay you know, I had her wrong after our first meeting. Bit like you really… you know, better for knowing.'

The inspector looked at her, raised an eye brow and said.

'I suggest you leave now detective while you can still walk…'

She grinned at Nita as she stood to leave the little office.

'Yes boss.'

Returning to her own desk she gathered some papers and started to work through them. A little while later Allen Syms came into the office.

'Whoa the wanderer returns…' he said, 'well are you staying or going to join the ranks of the elite?'

She smiled, 'Staying.'

He looked up quickly.

'Really… I didn't expect that I thought you'd jump at that post, I'm really surprised.'

She nodded, 'I thanked them for the opportunity but it's seven years since 'Hawkeye' and to be honest I'm more of a grass roots copper. I like the nitty gritty from the streets, I don't think I'd be happy with all that electronic high tech stuff, it's a young coppers game. The old man wasn't too pleased mind but hey it was my decision in the end, I'm happy it's sorted now and I can get back to moving on… you know what I mean Alan.'

He nodded and set about updating her on some case developments then the two of them condensed the two sets of papers and worked together adding the bits of information he'd returned with.

Chapter Twelve

Nita could hear the phone ringing as she got to the front door, Juggling the two shopping bags she was carrying and trying to find her keys for the door in her handbag she finally crashed into the small hallway and staggered into the living room just as the phone fell silent, 'Sod it!' She uttered and calmly now, took the shopping bags into the kitchen. Picking up the extension phone she back-tracked the number and called it, it rang a few times then was answered.

'Who is it?' a child's voice said.

She grinned replying. 'Nani… who are you?'

'Elizabeth.'

'Someone has just tried to call me Elizabeth do you know who that might have been?'

'No.'

'Okay, will you go and find mummy or daddy sweetheart.'

'Okay.'

The line went dead, Nita chuckled replaced the handset and waited. A few minutes later it rang.

'Hello,' she said.

'Hello you too, how are you?'

Angus's soft voice said; his gentle Scottish tones warmed her as they did to everyone he spoke to.

'I'm fine, your secretary found you then?' she said laughing softly.

'Aye, she's taken it upon herself to answer the phone whenever she can, it's a race sometimes if we are expecting a work call or something like that. Mind you she's very effective in dealing with all these cold call and automated systems, she can get them really flustered sometimes.'

Nita laughed aloud this time then asked.

'Have one of you called me a few minutes ago? I was just back from the shops and couldn't juggle two bags and open the door so missed you.'

'Yes, Em wanted a word, she's spoken to Robert Graham and sorted something out about *Finbar*. She's talking to Richard just now so I'll get her to give you a call when she's done okay? this with Richard could go on for a while you know.'

'Fine, I'm home now and not going anywhere so any time will do. Give the twins a hug and kiss from Nani Angus. Love to everyone, bye.'

It was over an hour before Emma called back, she downloaded the conversation she'd had with Robert Graham and then this evening's call with Richard to arrange what they'd decided to do with *Finbar* and how Mr G was going to help them. Emma wanted to know how the meeting had gone with her old boss and how he'd taken her decision not to join the new team. She laughed when Nita told her of his reaction to the news adding.

'Oh very churlish that, you'd have thought he'd have been more mature about it, doesn't set a good example to the team when the boss spits his dummy out.'

They both laughed now before Emma said.

'Right, so when Robert gets back to us we'll sort a weekend out and meet at the Grahams, you alright with that?'

'Yes, fine. Take care Em give the twins my love and we'll speak soon. Lots of love…bye'

Nita unpacked the shopping, made herself a light dinner and settled in the small living room for the evening. She called Louise for a chat and discovered that their other housemate would be away this coming weekend so decided some 'therapeutic' shopping was needed arranging to spend the Saturday together. Having spoken to Lou it came to mind that it had been a few weeks since she'd even spoken to Harold let alone been to see him as she'd promised and as she was generally feeling much stronger and in control of her emotions, it was about time she made the effort to go to York to see him and decided that that would be Sundays plan. Locking the house up, she made a drink and padded off to bed.

'Hi where abouts are you?'

Nita heard Emma ask Angus then repeat his answer.

'We're about 20 minutes away he says, but to be honest Nita we are coming a completely different way than dad used to, I don't recognise any of these roads. Have you heard from Nan and granddad yet?'

'Yes, they're on their way from Portbridge, we'll meet them at the Grahams yard.'

'Great, see you soon.'

Nita turned off the road into the narrow lane that led to the Grahams car park, parking nose into the hedge she started to unload the boot of the car. As she set off to walk down to the yard and pontoons she turned as a car horn sounded and saw Mary and Richards's car pulling into the parking area. They hugged one another and began to empty their car of hold-alls. Mary pulled a shopping trolley out of the boot and loaded their bags onto it. Nita looked at Richard and raised an eye-brow, he grinned and pointing first to his head then his feet said.

'Up here for thinking down there for dancing… if it's labour saving then there's nothing you can't teach her!'

Mary turned, looked at Richard then Nita and said.

'Problem…? Can you carry this lot all that way down to the boat… hhmmm?' she looked from one to another, 'No thought not, now grab something and let's get this boat on the water!'

Laden with their bags and bedding they finally staggered to a breathless halt at the top of the first ramp to the pontoons where they deposited everything on the ground, breathing a sigh of relief and shaking some feeling back into their arms pleased they'd made it. Behind them Nita heard a chuckle then the familiar voice of Robert Graham.

'Whey Jamie lad thars just seen the best example of Sherpa's thars every likely to see this side of the Himalaya's son, hee hee hee.'

He stood up as Nita walked towards him and returned the hug she gave him.

'Hello pet, good to see you, I must say you're looking a lot more alive than last time I saw you.'

She grinned and nodded.

'Day by day Robert, work in progress you could say. Emma and I have helped eachother getting this far and yes, the family have been amazing too. I think you've met Richard before but this Mary his wife.'

'Hello pet.' Robert said and held his hand out to her. As she shook it he said.

'We did meet a few years ago when Stephen brought Finbar up for the first time. Good to see you again, I'm sorry the circumstance aren't better.'

Mary smiled and shook his hand warmly, 'Thank you.'

'Right,' he said, 'this is going to be very strange to watch *Finbar* sail off once more after so many years wintering here. She's on one of the lower pontoons all ready to go. We checked over the engines and she's got enough fuel. We emptied the fresh water tanks, sterilized them and half-filled them again. You just need to load your gear and you're away.'

He turned to Nita.

'Maggie wondered if you and Emma would pop up to the hoose before you leave pet alright. Where is the lass any roads, leaving you all to do the work!'

'NO I'm not, I'm here!'

Everyone turned to see Emma and Angus walking towards them laden with supermarket bags. As they drew near to the group she put her bags down and walked to Robert. He pulled her into a body smothering embrace. As they eventually parted she reached out and rested her hand on his arm, his face looked strained his eyes sad.'

'I was intending to see her before we leave anyway.'

He nodded and taking a deep breath said softly.

'Whey pet just look at you, you were nothing but a shrimp when you forst came to the yard Emma. A puff of wind would have blown you over, and now… whey they'd both be so proud of now hinny.'

He caught a breath in his throat for a moment, paused, regained his composure and continued.

'Right, Jamie son grab something and let's get this on the boat.'

When everything was on-board *Finbar* Robert, Emma and Nita left the family and made their way up to the house. As they approached the gate Nita stopped, looked around and said to Robert.

'I so expected Sally to come hurtling over the wall.'

She looked at Robert to see him shaking his head.

'Nay lass we lost her more than a year ago, mind we got her a companion before she went but this one's impossible… bit like your dad pet… selective hearing if tha knows what l mean…! If ahve nothing better to do you know!'

As they approached the house door they heard excited barking coming from inside and bumping on the door, Robert shouted and all the noise stopped. He opened the door and the girls saw a young Border Colley staring at them its head cocked to one side and its tail wagging just like Sally's used to.

'This is Barney, a 20 month old hooligan!'

Barney approached the group sniffing his way around them as Robert removed his hat and coat calling out.

'They're here Maggie love.' to the girls he said, 'Sit yersels down, we'll have a brew.'

Maggie Graham came from an adjoining room into the large kitchen area. Both Emma and Nita stood as she approached and the three of them shared a collective embrace then in her soft highland tone she asked softly.

'How are you two, are you managing to be getting on with things?

Disengaging herself from the embrace she looked from one to the other, searching their faces for an answer, the girls smiled and nodded, Nita said.

'Day to day really,' she shrugged glancing at Emma, 'we talk a lot and share how each day has been.'

Emma smiled, 'I have Angus and the twins to distract me but even then there are moments when something comes at me all of a rush, you know?'

Mrs G nodded, 'Aye aye it happens, it will get easier in time. Sit you down, we'll have some tea.'

Almost an hour later Robert, Emma and Nita walked along the pontoon to where *Finbar* was moored her engines quietly drumming away. Leaving Maggie Graham at the house for this last time had been emotional especially for Emma after the years she'd known the Grahams and their boatyard quietly tucked away in this backwater and for Nita also. Everyone was gathered either on the pontoon or on the boat ready to leave. Giving Robert one final embrace they boarded *Finbar* and as Jamie and Mr G slipped the lines they motored away from the yard; just now it would have been possible to almost touch the overwhelming sense of emotion everyone was feeling. There were no words spoken for quite some time as everyone processed some particular memory recalled from past journey's started here at the beginning of each new year's planned cruises. Emma sat close to Angus resting her head on his shoulder, his arm around her protectively. Nita took herself up to the flying bridge and sat behind Richard at the helm. She turned to look back towards the yard as they turned the slight bend on the canal. She smiled remembering the very first time she saw the yard appear to her as they rounded the bend. That was the first weekend her relationship with Stephen began, she remembered her surprise that there could possibly be a boat yard this far from the sea in the heart of the countryside.

'How are you doing Nita?'

Richard said, glancing over his shoulder at her, she looked at him for a few moments.

'Honestly…' she paused, 'empty, I've got no more tears to cry I just feel empty, hollow.'

'Oh Nita I'm so sorry. Mary and I just feel so helpless, we just wish we could do more for you and Emma. I know it's hard to believe right now but time will help it to become bearable. Not that you'll ever forget and the loss will still feel so raw sometimes but you'll find a way of coping. The twins will help you know, as they grow they'll come closer to you as their Nani. Anyway, enough now, just I'm so sorry.'

It took some time for this sombre cloud that hung over them to clear, helped mainly when Mary delivered drinks and food for them all. From the flying bridge Richard said quietly to Nita as she went to join the others in the saloon.

'Never ceases to amaze me even after 42 years, she knows just what's going to lift everyone's spirits. Come and relieve me when you've eaten.'

She nodded, 'I will.'

That break seemed to motivate everyone and after the lunch, boxes and bags were broken out and the task of clearing all the cupboards and lockers began in earnest.

Nita had gone to relieve Richard on the bridge and spent time while helming *Finbar* contemplating the last seven years she'd spent with Stephen. Bits of passing scenery reminding her of special moments; like the optical effect a ploughed field had or the light filtering through a copse of trees, and then the challenge of the first swing bridge.

'Heads up below, Swing Bridge coming up.'

She called and manoeuvred to the bank. From below came the sound of people rushing around and raised voices. Five minutes elapsed before Emma and Angus climbed onto the tow path to walk to the bridge gently pushing and prodding one another and giggling. The air of hilarity continued as they opened the bridge and waited for Nita to pass through. She'd just closed to the bank again to wait for them when a shriek and hysterical laughter caused her to spin round to look back to the bridge just in time to see Angus picking himself up off the ground and Emma doubled over laughing hysterically. Leaving the helm she slipped down the stairs to the saloon just as the couple climbed back onto Finbar, Emma gasping for breath unable to speak. Mary and Richard looked on quite concerned that one of them was hurt asking what had happened.

Angus began to explain that he'd slipped on the cobble pathway which sent Emma back into hysterics again. Pointing and laughing at the same time she said, between gasps.

'I told him to mind the duck poo as we opened it but he'd forgotten when we started to close it and….he….' The rest was lost in an incoherent garble.

Not looking too happy Angus said quietly.

'I'm going to change out of these trousers, have we got a rubbish bag l can put them in?' Mary followed him down to the galley.

Emma had calmed down when he came back into the saloon, she went to him and tried to hug him but he half-heartedly resisted her however, she persevered until he allowed her to give him a big hug and a kiss.

'I'm sorry,' she said, 'but that was so funny.'

All calm and focused again on continuing the clear-up with Richard back on the helm, Nita then joined in sorting stuff to keep or discard. Emma appeared some time later holding a hard-backed book and sat on the long settee.

'What have you found sweetheart?' Angus asked.

'It's the boats log, I never knew Dad had kept one but look it's from that very first cruise we took.'

She looked up at Mary and Richard.

'Do you remember that first cruise when we sailed up the Loch to Fort William?'

Emma opened it and began scrolling through the pages reading odd entries and giggling from time to time. Mary sat beside her gently stroking her back and looking over her shoulder, Richard returned to the helm and set them back on their way again. After a while Emma looked up at Nita.

'Hey, you're in here; he's written about the day of the attack and being in hospital and meeting you.

Thought you were compassionate and found it hard to believe a person like that could be a hard faced detective like your boss.'

The three women laughed briefly at the tone of the entry. Emma closed the book and stood up.

'Do you know what, I'm going to write up this last trip then we've got a record of all our trips on *Finbar*.'

All through the afternoon as they continued down the canal, cupboards were emptied into boxes or clothes and bedding were bagged up, and a pile of stuff began to grow by the patio doors ready to off-load when they arrived at the Marina. It was growing quite dark as they approached the canal side pub that Stephen and Nita had stopped at on that first weekend together. Richard brought them, gently, alongside the bank and after a brief discussion Angus was dispatched to see if the pub was open and serving food, if it was then they could stay here for the night. Appearing from the door onto the towpath some time later he gave them the thumbs up then disappeared back into the pub. Having moored Finbar up, Nita, Emma, Richard and Mary walked to the pub to join Angus. Much much later with a watery moon subtly lighting their way along the towpath they walked and staggered a little back to the boat and shortly afterwards settled down for the night.

The morning started slowly and quietly where options of a full English breakfast or elements of it supported by strong coffee or tea helped some of them gather their heads together and focus on the day's tasks. Richard left them, going up to the bridge and started one of the engines.

'Ready to cast off please.'

Nita and Emma went and released the mooring lines, once back on-board they found it really difficult to motivate themselves, there was a definite lack of enthusiasm to get on or do anything. Emma said quietly.

'Will it be alright if I go and write up the log from yesterday?'

'Don't see why not.' Nita replied, 'No-one seems to have the energy to do anything right now.'

Emma nodded and went down to sit at the plotting table in the corner of the galley. She opened the book at the last entry; from last summer's cruise up the east coast of Scotland and on the next page the journey up to the Grahams yard for the winter just passed. She studied the list of jobs dad wanted Robert Graham or himself with Nita to do while *Finbar* was out of the water. She read and re-read the list in his handwriting; while it made her feel quite emotional, she found reading the list brought her close to him. After a while she began to write, filling in the details first:

Place of Departure

Destination

Course

Weather Forecast (Wind, Sea state)

Crew.

She began to write;

Date 29/04

Time 1130

Place of Departure

Left the Grahams yard on Finbar for the last time. It's been 15 years since we took Finbar up there for the first time, I was just a little girl then, now I'm a mum. It's been like a second home for me and dad all this time. The Grahams, Robert and Maggie have been like substitute grandparents to me. I'm going to miss them, it's not going to be the same.

Destination

We are taking Finbar down to the Estuary Marina where hopefully she is to be sold. We've all talked about what is the best thing to do with her as we haven't been cruising in the summer like we used to do. The past 5 years we've practically circumnavigated the whole of the English coastline. Mind you we've anchored in some amazing bays and harbours and discovered some beautiful 'back-waters'.

Made good time down towards Portbridge, moored up at a canal side pub for the night. Apparently dad and Nita stopped here the weekend they got together. Good food, good atmosphere a very welcoming place, we had a good night.

Course

Down the canal to the Marina on the estuary.

Weather

Grey and chilly leaving the Grahams, west or south-west breeze made it feel colder. Kind of reflected how we all felt I think, better as we got down towards the pub.

Barometer 990

Crew

Me, Angus, Mum Dad and Nita.

Just after lunch they worked through the big Severn Trent lock; by the time they were out of the lock onto the river they were almost hysterical with laughter as Nita relayed to them her first impressions of this formidable structure and how angry she'd been with Stephen. An hour or so later they passed the field where the drama began that led to her meeting Stephen for the first time.

Angus was helming up on the flying bridge, everyone else was busy continuing packing things into boxes from the galley cupboards and the bar cupboard in the saloon. Emma touched Nita on the shoulder.

'Got a minute?'

She sat on one of the long settees patting the cushion next to her for Nita to sit.

'You alright?' Nita said as she sat beside her.

'Fine, I want to ask, no suggest perhaps, and say what you feel Nita but be honest, okay?'

Nita looked at Emma curiously wondering what was coming next. 'Okay, yes,' she said and waited.

'If we make Portbridge this evening and can moor up at the old wharf for the night, I'd like to scatter dads' ashes on the water tomorrow, would you be okay with that? I've spoken to Angus about it and he said I should talk to you.'

Surprised, Nita studied Emma for a while struggling to process what she'd just suggested rationally; trying not to become too emotional.

'Why Em, I mean why at Portbridge, aren't there other places that carry memories of dad?'

Emma nodded, 'Yes but Portbridge held great memories for him as well. I mean that was the beginning of you giving me back the dad I'd known before mum died… and Portbridge especially the wharf was significant to you as well. Think about it and let me know,' she reached to hold Nita's arm, 'but be honest with me and yourself, okay.'

Nita smiled and nodded. They embraced briefly, stood up and

carried on with the sorting out of stuff to take with them or to ditch.

'Em, Nita, got a minute.'

Richard called from the flying bridge. They both made their way up the steps onto the bridge shivering as they emerged.

'Flipping heck it's chilly up here, are you okay granddad?' Emma said.

'Yeah I'm fine, look we're coming up to Portbridge, are we stopping?'

The two girls stood arms folded tightly hugging themselves to keep warm.

'Yes.' Emma said, 'If we can moor up at the wharf, we'll stay here tonight and get something to eat in town. Where did you and dad used to go, was it the Duchess or something like that?'

Nita nodded, 'Yes but I'd heard it had closed. We can always go for an Indian, there's one going into town that used to be quite good.'

Twenty minutes later, wrapped up in warm coats this time, they were moored up at the old wharf standing together looking at two new smart apartment blocks standing where the old NCB offices once stood. The developers had even built some raised flower beds and placed some benches and a few tables around the area for people to sit and enjoy the view across the river. Nita nodded approvingly, she had to agree the apartments looked very prestigious, each with a balcony overlooking the wharf with views across the river and fields. She smiled, they'd even kept the rusty old crane on the wharf side as a feature. It had been cleaned up a bit and surrounded with some railings now on which was a plaque had been placed relating to the history of the original site.

Quite a lot of memories came flooding back at her as she looked around the wharf, like where Mick Holmes's office had stood and where she'd first set eyes on Stephen. She turned and looked back at *Finbar* remembering what a state she'd been in the night she was vandalised and how this Stephen Leigh-Grace had looked after being attacked. Then again, she smiled to herself shivering ever so slightly as she felt a subtle rush of excitement recalling the September when she'd accepted his invitation to travel up to the Grahams yard with him and the passion they'd generated that led them into their love affair and time together. Suddenly she decided what she wanted to do about Emmas' offer, she turned, reached out and touched Ems' shoulder.

'Em I've decided, yes let's do it!'

Emma reached for her hand, squeezed gently and smiled. 'Good, tomorrow then.'

'Right, did someone say something about food, 'cause I'm ravenous!' Richard said.

'Nothing new there then.' Mary said quietly.

A ripple of laughter circulated through the group as they walked through the garden area out on to the roadside path that led towards the Duchess and Portbridge. It was clear as they approached the Duchess that the pub was closed, they could clearly see that it was enveloped in scaffolding. Standing at the foot of the steps waiting for them were Louise and Alan Syms and Moira who they'd arranged to join them for the evening.

'It's closed!' Alan said as they stood beside them. They surveyed the steps leading up to the original ornate entrance where a large sign read. CLOSED FOR REDEVELOPMENT.

'Let's hope they keep the character of the building.' Richard said.

Angus sort of huffed, 'You tell that to Weatherspoon's… mind you, if it's listed then they're going to have to retain a lot of its character.'

'Oh well,' Richard said, 'Curry or taxi into town?'

In the end they all trooped towards town where they shared an excellent selection of Asian food before returning to *Finbar* for drinks and other refreshments and having seen Louise Moira and Alan into a taxi turned in for the night.

Day three began with them gathered together on *Finbars* sun deck, they slipped the moorings turned *Finbar* around and motored into the centre of the river. Richard brought her to a stop so she was bow into the current feathering the throttles to hold her position as. Emma stood with Angus holding the box containing Stephens' ashes, she reached out for Nita to come beside her and together they tipped the contents over the side of the boat onto the rivers surface while Louise and Moira threw red white and yellow roses onto the surface. They all stood watching the current sweep them away some sinking below the surface. No-one spoke for quite some time, Emma turned and embraced Angus tightly reaching for Nita to come into the embrace as well.

'Bye dad,' she said, 'love you… miss you.'

Nita began to cry silently, her eyes just streamed tears. Louise took her into an embrace speaking quietly into her ear, she listened, nodding occasionally. Mary appeared through the patio doors with a tray of drinks.

'Not sure what you all wanted so there's a selection of spirits and tea.' she said quietly.

Richard called from the bridge.

'Can I take us back to the wharf now?'

'Yes,' Angus replied, 'all done now.'

A little later and all moored up at the wharf again they all sat around the sun deck quietly reminiscing about past holiday voyages. Alan, Louise and Moira stayed with them until the early afternoon before leaving, taking Richard with them to be dropped off at Asda to do a bit of shopping. He returned a couple of hours later with that evening's dinner.

'Steak!' Mary said as she rooted through the bag commenting.

'You decided on tonight's dinner then.'

Grinning he replied.

'Well I thought we'd eat here on board, just a quiet family dinner.'

The afternoon was spent quietly, there was a strange mood of peace and calm about the boat since they'd spread Stephens ashes. Everyone felt that this morning's events had brought final closure to his passing and now was the time to move on. As dusk fell the galley table was all laid out for an evening of fine dining. Mary, placing 2 bottles of wine in the centre of the table asked Richard to call everyone. Making a trumpet shape with his hands he stood in the door to the saloon and made a sound like a bugle.

'Dtuladatu…didididdee…dadadatur… call to mess for all crew!'

Mary stood in the galley, hands on hips, shaking her head slowly but couldn't help a broad grin.

'I really worry about you, you know; I think you're losing it sometimes!'

He grinned back at her however, his bugle call had the desired effect and a jolly 'crew' settled for dinner. Prawn cocktail, Fillet steak with fries and vegetables or salad and finally a cheese board with a selection of crackers. All this was accompanied by wine and from somewhere Richard produced a bottle of Port to go with the cheese and biscuits, commenting as he placed it in the middle of the table.

'You know we've almost drunk the cellar dry!'

Folding her arms across her tummy and blowing her lips out, Emma said.

'My compliments to the chef on the behalf of the whole crew, yet again you have managed to produce a banquet for us from such a tiny galley, thank you nan.'

While everything was cleared away at the end of the dinner Emma sat at the plotting table and wrote up the log for the last 2 days.

Date 30/04

Time 1030

Place of Departure

Left the Bargee and Farriers Arms, one of dads' watering holes when he was moving Finbar. It was a good night, strange with lots of memories of past trips shared but a good night. All slept well, had a good breakfast.

Destination

Aiming to at least make Portbridge tonight. (There's something I'd like to do whilst we are there.)

Course

As before

Weather

Much the same as yesterday if not a little milder.

Barometer 1005

Crew

No changes… 'We haven't had to throw anybody overboard yet!!!'

Date 31/04

Time 0930

Place of Departure

We made Portbridge last night and moored at the old NCB wharf. The whole site has been re-developed into smart apartments now. Funny, the only thing remaining that relates to its former life is a rusty old digger that the builders left as a feature. Met Alan and Louise Syms and Moira for the evening. We were going to go to the Duchess for a reunion meal but that's closed for refurbishment! We ended up having a curry, still good night.

This morning everyone met at the boat. I spoke to Nita and then announced that l wanted to spread dads' ashes here on the water. It was a special place for him; where he met Nita and l thought it would be nice to share it with her. Thinking about it now, l feel I've closed a cover on a book… a truly dreadful one and I'm ready to start something else now; l hope Nita sort of feels the same. Had a lovely family dinner tonight, Nan really does work miracles in that tiny galley.

Destination

Estuary Marina

Course

There is only one really… down-stream.

Weather

Still grey for May but warm

Barometer 1005

Crew

All of the family plus 3. Glad we were all together today. We've all suffered in one way or another with dads passing, we supported each other today. I think today has drawn a line under the past months and we can all start to look forward now.

Day four began quite later, no-one seemed in a rush to get on with the day. Once Richard had returned the galley bed to the dining area again, Mary got on and produced breakfast. It was getting on for midday when they slipped their lines and allowed *Finbar* to drift into the centre of the river under gentle propulsion. They all gathered on the bridge to take a last look at the old wharf and the view of Portbridge from the water something they would be unlikely to see again. Just as when they'd left the Grahams yard on Thursday the atmosphere at this moment was very sombre as everyone went through their personal reminiscences of the wharf and its significance in their lives. Nita sat quietly in the sundeck area watching the distance grow between them and the wharf as they motored round the bend in the river; she dabbed tears from her eyes with a tissue. She was aware that someone was sitting beside her now gently caressing her shoulder.

'Are you alright Nita, this must be so hard just now.'

She glanced over her shoulder to see Emma sitting beside her looking concerned. She gave her a half smile and stroked her leg in response.

'Mmm… it is but we have to get on with things don't we? Thank you for yesterday Em that really helped bring all of us some closure to the last year.'

'Well I couldn't sleep the other night at the pub thinking about stuff and decided the wharf was the best place to spread dads ashes, after all that was where it all started for you two and it was somewhere that meant a lot to him, he'd talk about when we were away before we all got know you and you started cruising with us.'

They sat together for quite some time lost in their own thoughts, recalling memories of time spent with Stephen. Mary appeared through the patio doors with a tray of drinks and biscuits.

'The boys are up top so I thought I'd come and sit with you two for a while, is that alright?'

They all shuffled around getting comfortable then shared the drinks and continued reminiscing about past holidays.

Later in the afternoon they were sailing down the widening estuary of what was now the river Ouse, approaching the Marina where *Finbar* was to be put up for sale. They moored up to a pontoon and Emma, Angus and Nita wove their way through a variety of yachts and motor cruisers on trailers and laid out in neat rows towards an office block. As they rounded the end of the building making their way to the main entrance laid out in front of them were some more yachts and cruisers on show to passing traffic on the main road. At the reception desk in a brightly lit foyer they introduced themselves asking to see a Mr Arthur Duncombe. After waiting a few minutes a man came from an office on the first floor, descended some steps and walked towards them. Tall and slim, his youthful looks belied his age; Nita thought he was probably in his mid-fifties.

'Afternoon, are you people Robert Graham has told me about? He filled me in on some of the circumstances about selling your boat. Can I just say I'm very sorry for your loss and if I can I'll do my best to advise you or act for you in selling the boat?'

They stood and the man shook hands with each of them, Emma replied.

'Thank you, yes Robert thinks you are the best person to talk to.'

Arthur smiled, 'He's a bit of a character don't you think, a one off? Salt of the earth though, what he doesn't know about boats can be written on a postage stamp and his wife is just so lovely. Robert and my late father used to have some fiery exchanges from time to time but remained friends until dad passed away. He was a great help to me when l took over the ropes and pulleys here.' He smiled briefly. 'Have you know him long?'

Emma said, 'I was eight the first year we took *Finbar* up to the Grahams yard. It sort of became a second home to me, a great play area. I grew up thinking Robert and Mary were surrogate grandparents.'

Arthur chuckled then turned to the reception desk.

'Luce, if there are any calls, I've gone for the day I'll call them back tomorrow. I'm going down to the water, finish up and I'll see you in the morning.'

The young lady acknowledged Arthur and he turned back to the group.

'Right should we go and have a look at this boat of yours?'

As the group walked down to where *Finbar* was moored Arthur asked them about cruises they'd taken over the years, how the boat handled in different conditions, whether they'd had any problems over the years with the mechanics or electrics. He laughed when Nita related to him some of the conversations Robert Graham had had with Stephen each winter they'd taken her up to his yard.

'Listen,' he said, 'Over the years I've moved quite a number of Roberts boats on and never had a problem with their condition or reliability.'

'Will you start her up?'

With the engines running he sat at the helms position and wound the revs up and went to look over the stern. He turned to Emma standing by the helm.

'Reduce her to tick over.'

Waiting for the engines to settle he lifted the deck panels to look at the engine bay and studied it for a while before calling to Emma again.

'Giver her half ahead will you.'

After a minute or two he closed the 2 panels and climbed up to the bridge helm.

'Will you slip the lines please?'

A couple of minutes later they were heading seaward when he opened the throttles up and *Finbar* came up on a plane. Weaving from side to side he turned to look back, nodding he shut the throttles down to slow. Once the boat settled down he went through the gears into reverse and again nodded.

Turning to Richard who was perched on one of the settees he nodded.

'Will you take over and take us back to the pontoon.'

Richard took the helm and Arthur went back down to the saloon.

'I should have known really but I had to put her through her paces. She's fine, Robert has worked his magic again. If you'd like to leave her with me I've got some people on my books who may well be interested in her.'

He casually ran his hand gently over the coving surrounding the helm position. Emma looked at Angus then Nita.

'Can you give us any idea of her value?'

'Mmmm tricky, she's old but sound and very clean all through. They've changed some specifications, modernising her fit and re-shaping some of her superstructure. That said the re-fit after she was trashed will help plus, Roberts magic touch I think I could well get top book. If I can get a bidding war going that would make a huge difference. Bottom line, I should be able to get 7 to 9000, does that sound fair?'

Angus asked now.

'What will you take?'

Arthur grinned and replied jovially.

'I don't know whose worse a Yorkshire man or a Scot, You and Robert G are cut from the same cloth.

I usually take 20% but this time and trying to avoid an irate phone call from a certain Geordie 12½ %.'

Emma reached out and squeezed Angus's arm to stop a response from him.

'Can we all talk about it and let you know in the morning?'

'Certainly, are you staying on board tonight? If so, there's a nice eating place 100 yards from our main gate.'

Emma replied, 'Thank you but we're going to eat here tonight.'

Arthur smiled, 'Sort of the last supper perhaps.'

Emma looked around at everyone, smiled and said.

'Yeah, maybe.'

He nodded, 'Quite understand well, have a good night I'll see you tomorrow.'

He stepped onto the pontoon and looking back at them waved and walked back through the boat yard to the office.

Having eaten dinner they sat around the table in the galley until late in the evening discussing why to accept Arthur Duncombes offer to help sell *Finbar* and then the reasons not to. Everyone knew that there really was only one conclusion but no one wanted admit it or be the first to accept that his offer and terms was going to be the answer. In the end common sense prevailed and they all agreed to leave it to him. Decision made they all adjourned to the saloon to watch television while Richard made up the galley berth for the last time. When he returned to the saloon, Emma excused herself.

'Just going to write up the log and then bed I think.'

'Yeah,' Angus responded, 'I'm not really concentrating on this, give me a call when you've written it up and I'll come and join you.'

Mary and Richard nodded agreeing. 'Yes us too I think.' Mary added.

Emma left them and went to the chart table, pulling the log book from its pigeon hole she opened it.

Date 01/05

Time 1030

Place of Departure

We slipped the moorings around 1040 this morning. It was all a bit emotional for us all, especially Nita given the years she and dad met here to begin runs up to the Grahams or bring Finbar down ready to start another years cruising. Made the estuary marina in plenty of time and met Arthur Duncombe as arranged through Robert. Nice man, absolutely straight with us about Finbar, her age, fit out etc. He took her out into the estuary and literally rang her out then told us how much she was worth. We've all sat tonight discussing it and decided to let him handle the sale. (Robert did say he was a straight talker and would do the best for us.) We'll speak to Arthur tomorrow and then say our farewell to her. I'll write up the last entry from home.

Destination

Here, the Estuary Marina

Course

Weather

Still grey and overcast. Scenery from Portbridge has been lovely, very rural and arable.

Barometer 988 rain

Crew

All still together for this last night on board.

9am and they all walked through the boat yard up to Arthur's office. The receptionist smiled as they walked into the showroom.

'Morning, Mr Duncombe is expecting you, I'll show you to the conference room if you'd like to follow me, there's tea and coffee available if you'd like to help yourselves, he'll be with you directly.'

'Thank you.' Emma responded.

Richard set about making drinks for everyone and Arthur Duncombe appeared a little later.

'Morning,' he said walking into the room, 'how are we all this morning, my guess is you didn't have a restful night, yes?'

There were nods and smiles all round as Emma replied.

'There was a lot to talk about after you'd left us but, at the end of the day, we all think the best solution is to leave the sale to you. Everything of ours is packed ready to just load into a van, we just need to know what you need from us?'

'Right, do you have the original factory manifest or was that missing when you bought *Finbar*?'

Emma rooted through a folder of papers and eventually withdrew a document handing it to Arthur.

'Excellent!' he exclaimed, 'that is so often missing when we sell a boat. It's like a passport and really difficult to get a copy. Additionally to this, are you leaving other stuff to be sold with the boat?'

Emma produced another piece of paper, glanced at it and passed it to Arthur. While he looked though it Emma explained.

'Granddad wrote this up as we came down to you, we all decided there wasn't any point in taking the tender and engine and other bits away to sell. Having all this extra kit on her might help sweeten the cost and seal the deal… you see where I'm coming from.'

'Ohh having this extra stuff will certainly do that, I'll add it to the advert. Now have you got a truck or van?'

Richard replied. 'No, we were going to ask if there was an Enterprise hire company near where we could get a one-way hire.'

'There is but I've got a van you can use and a couple of my guys will run you all back to Portbridge with everything.

An hour later all their bags and the bits were loaded into the Marina's van and an estate car. Emma and Nita walked hand in hand down to the pontoon *Finbar* was moored at. They sat together for a while in the sun deck. They didn't say much just sat with their thoughts, they both shed a tear and consoled one another. Eventually returning to the front of the offices and the others, they said goodbye to Arthur. He reassured them he would keep them updated on any offers that might come in for *Finbar*.

The journey back to Portbridge was uneventful and having emptied the van and car they thanked Arthurs' two drivers for their help. They spent the evening quietly reflecting on the weekend and how it had touched each of them at one time or another remembering Stephen and travelling on the canal or away around the South coast and over to Northern France. After breakfast on the Tuesday morning Emma and Angus took Richard and Mary to the station seeing them onto the train down to Poole before driving back to Bristol. Nita found herself alone again wandering around the house tidying things away. Sitting in the little living room she sighed and set about facing the thought of rebuilding a life on her own once again but with some amazing warm memories of love and passion, fun and laughter and a new, welcoming family that she felt close to and, very much part of.

Epilogue

Some 10 weeks after they'd left *Finbar* at the Estuary Marina, Arthur Duncombe called Emma.

'I've had an offer on the boat Emma, I managed to get three people interested in her and have an offer of £11,750. A bit of a plus for you on what I originally valued her at, is that acceptable?'

After a quick phone round the family, Emma called him back accepting the price. Within the week all the paperwork was signed off and a passage of family history closed, well almost!

It's almost eighteen months now since the family said goodbye to *Finbar ll* and the years of fun they'd all shared at one time or another initially cruising around the UK, then becoming more adventurous and pushing their horizons to include the Channel Islands and Northern France.

Emma, Angus and the twins have just parked in the main car park in Weston-Super-Mare on their way home after spending a bank-holiday weekend in Cornwall camping for the first time. While Emma was sorting out some snacks and drinks for them all, Angus wandered off towards the promenade. Coming across a small boat yard some distance from their car, he stood for some time looking at a boat on a launch frame on the slipway, he grinned, turned and made his way back to the car.

'Where did you wander off to?' Emma said casually.

'Just to have a look around. I'd like you to go and look at something sweetness.'

She looked at him, 'What?'

'No, just go and see.'

'Come on Angus, what am I to go and see!'

'Go and find out love.'

'Angus…!' she exclaimed, looked at him and realising she was going to have to go and see for herself.

'Ohhhh!' She said irritated and set off across the car park.

'Where's mummy gone?' Elisabeth said.

'Ohh just to look at something.' Angus replied.

'Can we go see too?'

'In a minute, just give mummy some space then we'll go.'

When she arrived at the gates to the boat yard, she just stood at first and stared, looking at the same boat Angus had seen. Slowly she approached her until, standing beside her she firstly put her hand on the hull and then rested her forehead there saying softly.

'Hello you.'

Looking up she saw the boats name on the bow, *Finbar ll.*

Someone spoke behind her making her start a little.

'Sorry love but you shouldn't be her, it's dangerous you know, health and safety and all that.'

She turned to see a young man probably in his twenties, wearing overalls watching her. Behind him at the gates she could see Angus with the twins watching her too.

'I'm sorry,' she said, 'this was my father's boat, our family boat; we spent 8 years cruising all over

the place. We sold her two years ago when my dad passed away. It's a bit of a surprise to see her here now, what's happening to her do you know?'

The man seemed to relax a little at Emma's explanation and replied.

'We're servicing her ready to sail over to one of the Loughs in Ireland. This family have bought her for family holidays and breaks.'

Emma nodded saying, 'They'll have a great time in her, and she's a lovely boat, safe in any kind of weather. Could my family come and see her…please? If you stay here it'll be alright won't it… just to have a look; Please?'

The man eventually succumbed to Emma's sad eyes and appeal. 'Okay just for a minute or two I suppose.'

Emma smiled at him, reached out and touched his arm, 'Thank you.' she said and waved for Angus to come. They stood by Finbar for a while lifting the twins up to touch her hull and see her name. Eventually Emma turned to the young man.

'Thank you it's been nice to see her again. If you see the new owners will you tell them how lovely she is and I hope they'll get as much fun and pleasure from her we all did.'

The man nodded, 'I will.' he said.

Returning to the car they set off to continue their journey home, once they were on the motorway Emma called Nita. It rang for some before she answered.

'Hey how are you?' Emma said.

'Oh hello, a bit of a surprise, I was going to call you tonight to see how your weekend had gone and how the twins had managed.'

'Yeah it was good thanks, I think we all enjoyed the outdoor bit, the fresh air bit and after the first night the twins slept like logs. It's a great way to meet people, there were some other young kids on the site and to be honest once our two realised where we were, they were quite happy to join the gang; Angus and I mixed with the other parents and kept an eye on them all. One thing though… I'm definitely a fair weather camper, couldn't cope if it was wet or cold! Those people are a different breed; I like my home comforts too much, mind you I'd consider a caravan better still a motorhome.'

Nita chuckled, 'Just after I started at Portbridge as a DC they sent a whole group of us on an adventure weekend, team building they said a sort of taster, like an outward bound or D of E thing you know. It was interesting watching how different people took to it.'

'Actually what I'm calling for, apart from saying hello is, we've just seen *Finbar*… she's in a yard in Weston. A family have bought her and they're servicing her ready to go across to Ireland. She still looks lovely.'

There was silence on the phone, Emma thought she'd lost the signal.

'Nita, you still there… Nita hello…'

She heard her now, heard an intake of air like a gasp. 'Nita, are you okay?'

After another short pause before Emma heard her say.

'Yes… yes' as she seemed to compose herself, 'I'm fine, you just caught me out that's all; that was something I wasn't expecting.'

'Nita are you okay?'

'Yes, I'm okay Em honestly.'

'What did you do this weekend?'

'Long weekends are always difficult Em it allows memories and thoughts to creep in. If I keep busy I avoid too much time thinking. I met Louise on Saturday, we trundled over to Leeds, shopped, ate and went to the pictures. I stayed over at hers and met her new house mate Sarah, she's very nice they seem to get on okay. Yesterday Moira and Rik called, she's pregnant by the way, only 12 weeks so early days yet, then came back here this morning. It's just that the house is so quiet…you know!'

Emma felt she picked up a sense of isolation, loneliness in Nita's voice.

'Listen, have you and consultation stuff on the go at the moment?'

'No.'

'Okay, so pack a bag, a big bag and come down to us. We'd love to see you and I definitely know two little ones who'd be all over you like a rash. Nita don't think about it just come!'

'Well… isn't that going to put you out having me under your feet?'

'No, come on… you know you'd be a great help.'

'Well,' Nita thought for a few moments, 'if you're sure, it would be lovely to see you all.'

'Good, the right decision.' Emma said.

'I'll come down at the weekend.

 As arranged Nita arrived Friday evening joining Emma, Angus and the twins for their evening meal. She stayed for some weeks this time, even managing to carry on some consultancy work on line from their house. After this temporary upset of seeing *Finbar* again, things settled down and as time went on Emma and Nita's personal sense of loss at Stephen's passing very slowly began to ease; just as the saying goes; time is a great healer.

There was one final thing to do to close the ships log. Weeks later, sometime in the very early hours Emma woke and laid for some time unable to fall asleep again. Quietly padding downstairs she made a mug of tea and sat at the breakfast bar. Something was pricking her conscience, suddenly she went to look for her laptop bag, and rooting through it she found the ships log. Reading the last two entries she found a pen and began to write.

Date 21/09

Time 0345

Place of departure

Destination

Course

Weather

Crew

N/B

I've left all this blank because we left Finbar at the Marina for the last time in May last year. I've discovered her new owners are to sail her over to Ireland. I really do hope they have as much fun and pleasure with her as we had over the years. This will be the last ever entry in the log, there was something dad used to say, to himself really, when we left Finbar on her mooring in Poole after our summer cruise. He said it was something that the Captain did when the boat had docked and everything was closed down. He used to ring the telegraph to 'Finished with engines.' So this is how I'm going to end this last entry.

Finished with Engines.